No Game No Life 1

YUU KAMIYA

IN THIS FANTASY WORLD, 'ERYTHING'S A GAME— AND THESE GAMER SIBLINGS LAY TO WIN!

"—Sora...
why do I
have to be
naked and
washing
Shiro's
hair?"

●REC

"...
Nggh...
Brother,
I hate
you."

"I won't give it to anyone. Our country belongs to us."

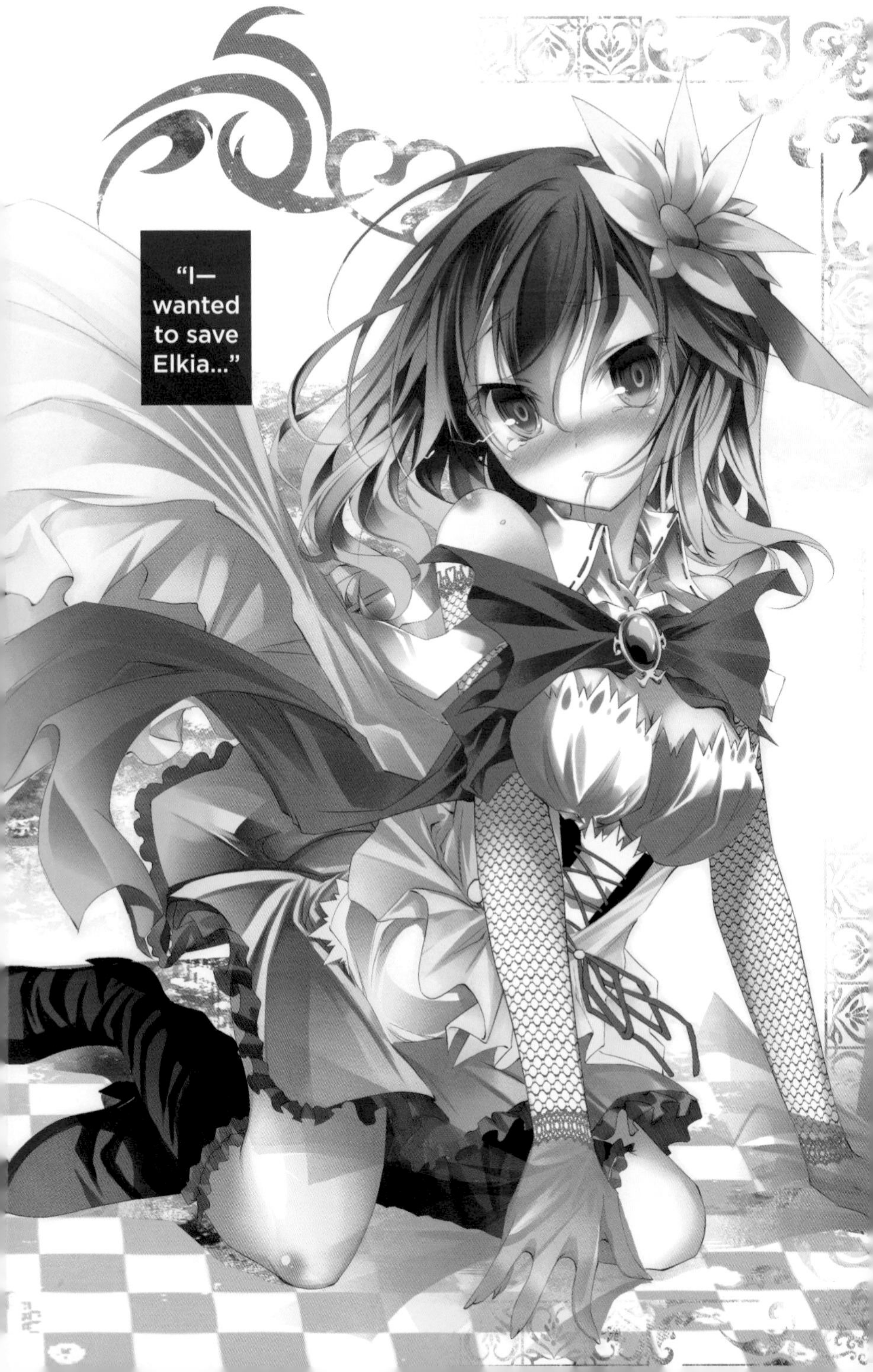
"I—
wanted
to save
Elkia..."

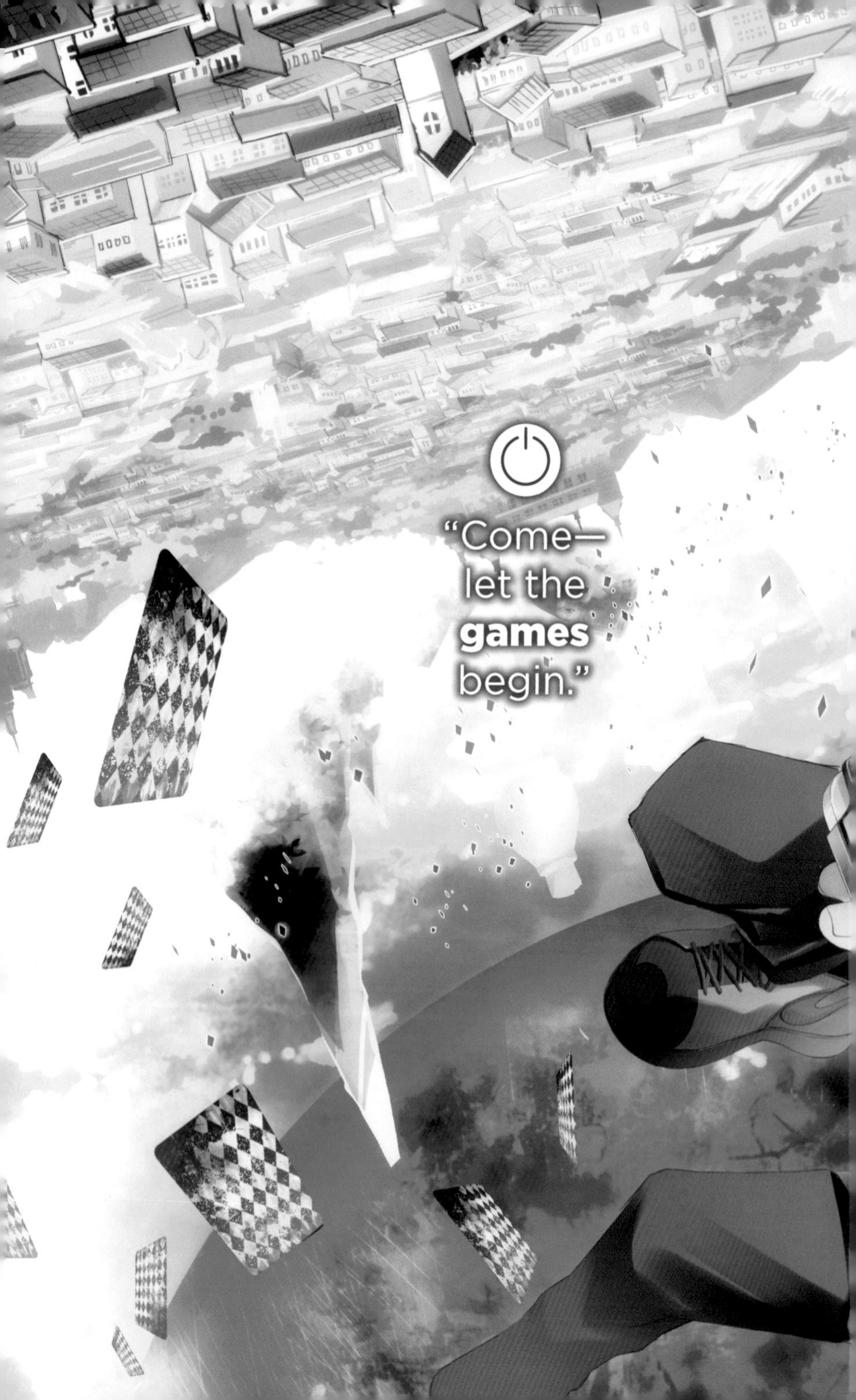
"Come—
let the
games
begin."

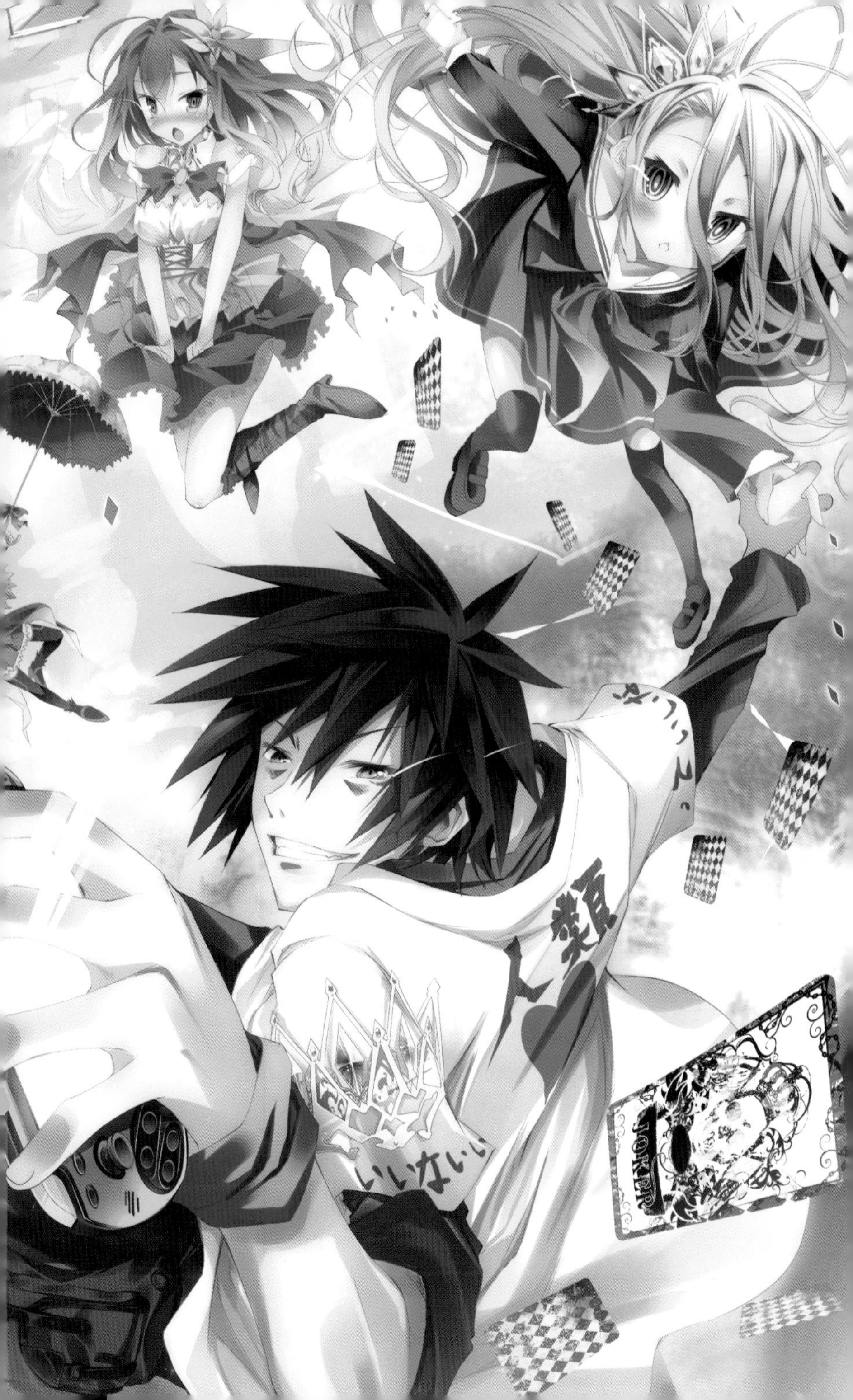
人類

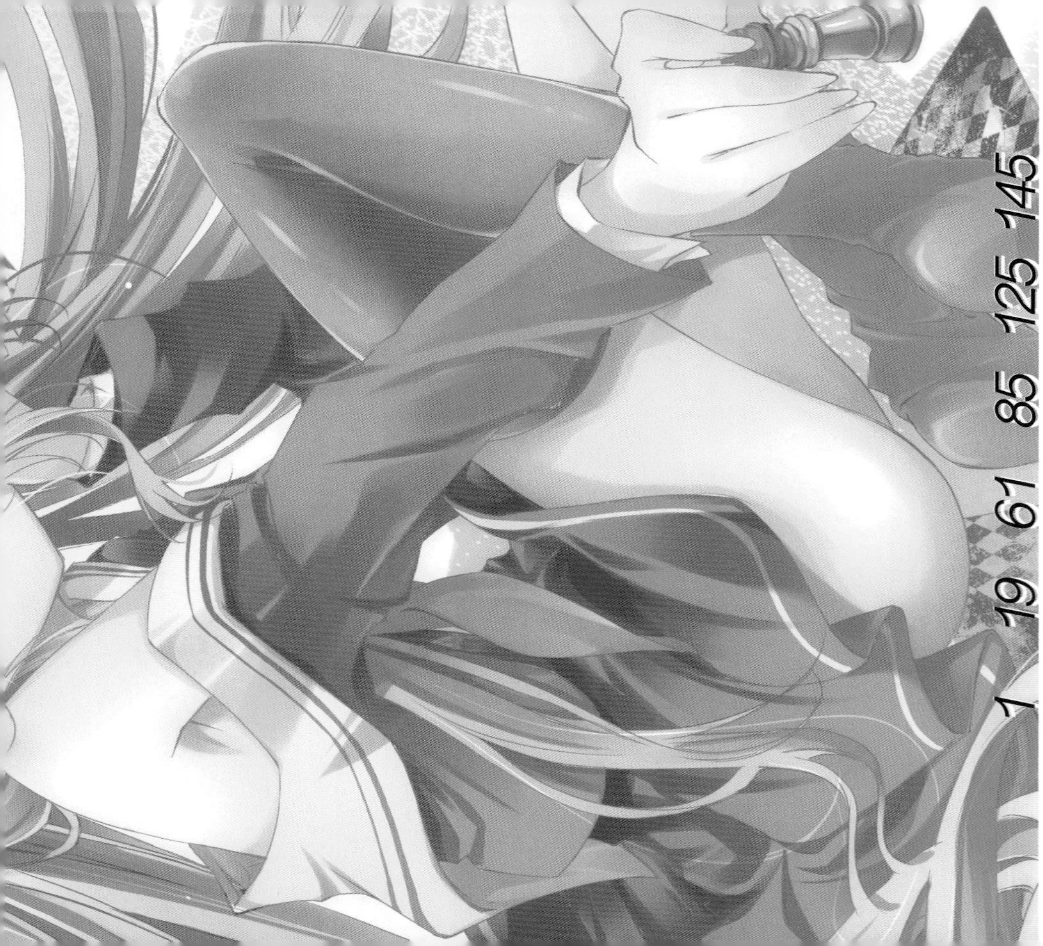

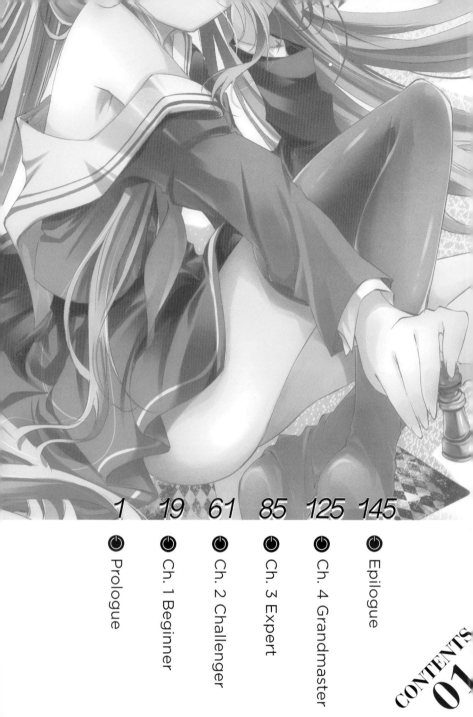

CONTENTS 01

No Game No Life

YUU KAMIYA

1

YEN ON

NEW YORK

NO GAME NO LIFE, Volume 1
YUU KAMIYA

Translation by Daniel Komen
Cover art by Yuu Kamiya

NO GAME NO LIFE Volume.1
©Yuu Kamiya 2012.
First published in Japan in 2012 by
KADOKAWA CORPORATION, Tokyo.
English translation rights
arranged with KADOKAWA
CORPORATION, Tokyo, through
Tuttle-Mori Agency, Inc., Tokyo.

Yen On
1290 Avenue of the Americas
New York, NY 10104

Visit us at yenpress.com
facebook.com/yenpress
twitter.com/yenpress
yenpress.tumblr.com
instagram.com/yenpress

First Yen On Edition: April 2015

Yen On is an imprint of Yen Press, LLC.
The Yen On name and logo are
trademarks of Yen Press, LLC.

The publisher is not responsible for
websites (or their content) that are
not owned by the publisher.

Library of Congress
Cataloging-in-Publication Data
Names: Kamiya, Yu, 1984– author,
   illustrator. | Komen, Daniel, translator.
Title: No game no life / Yuu Kamiya,
   translation by Daniel Komen.
Other titles: No gemu no raifu. English
Description: First Yen On edition. |
   New York, NY : Yen ON, 2015–
Identifiers: LCCN 2015041321 |
   ISBN 9780316383110 (v. 1 : pbk.)
Subjects: | BISAC: FICTION / Fantasy /
   General. | GSAFD: Fantasy fiction.
Classification: LCC PL832.A58645
   N6 2015 | DDC 895.63/6—dc23
LC record available at
   http://lccn.loc.gov/2015041321

ISBN: 978-0-316-38311-0

13

LSC-C

Printed in the
United States of America

⏻ PROLOGUE

—*Urban legends.* These whispers traveling through the world, as countless as the stars, represent a kind of *wish*.

—Like the urban legend that humans have never been to the moon.

—Like the Freemason conspiracy hidden in the dollar bill.

—Like the Philadelphia Experiment into time travel. The nuclear shelter on the Chiyoda Line, Area 51, the Roswell incident, etc.—

Looking at these innumerable urban legends, one can see a clear pattern emerging. Namely…they are composed of a *wish*: "It sure would be cool!" It's said that there's no smoke without fire. But when you think about the nature of rumors and how a big fish gets embellished until it's too big to even *be* a fish, you can see how these urban legends come to form. In short, *they're based on true stories but are not themselves true.* To put it bluntly, *they're mostly BS*. And yet they don't quite deserve to be complained about, or even wondered about, really. Since ancient times, people have always preferred fate over coincidence beginning with the very fact that *the birth of humanity was the product of astronomically unlikely coincidence*. Thus, people wanted to think, from their instincts, from the rules they had experienced, that *someone intentionally made humanity*. That the world was made not of chaos, but of order. Imagining someone in the back pulling the strings, to find meaning in an absurd and unreasonable world…at the very least, wishing that it could be true. So, too, can it be said that urban legends are generally another product of this earnest *wish*.

—So. There are *urban legends* numerous enough to light up the sky. What isn't as well known is that some of them are actually *true*.

—Just to be clear, this isn't to say that any of the previously mentioned urban legends are true. It's simply that there do exist urban legends emerging from a different principle.

—For instance, a *rumor* too surreal to believe becoming an *urban legend*.

Here is an example of such a *rumor*. It's a rumor, whispered around earnestly on the Internet, of a gamer named " " (Blank). They say he holds unbeatable records in the online rankings for over 280 games. That there's a gamer who's swept up all the world's top ranks with his player name " ". You probably think, "No way." Of course, that's what everyone thinks. The hypothesis they've come up with is simple:

That it's become a trendy convention among game devs to just leave their names as a space in the rankings for their games so people wouldn't know who they were, and it isn't an actual player—.

Yet, bizarrely, people keep on claiming that they've actually played him. They say he's unbeatable. They say he's shut out chess programs that have even beaten grandmasters. They say his play style defies common sense and is impossible to read. They say they used tools and cheat codes and they still lost. They say…they say…they say—.

Those who are even a little interested in such *rumors* probe deeper. Why? It's simple. If he has the top online ranks in console games, PC games, and social network games, then he must have an account. If he exists, then you should be able to look at his history. But there's no way such a person could actually—.

—And they sneer and search—and there's the trap. Because there actually is a user registered with the name " " on every console, on every SNS, and anyone can see " "'s history: and there can be found a number of trophies that could literally be expressed as "countless." Because " "'s *match records list not a single loss.*

—And so the plot thickens. Even though the facts are solid, the *rumor* becomes even more unbelievable.

"It's a hacker who's erased his loss records."

"It's a gamer group that invites only the best players."

—Etc., etc. Thus, a new *urban legend* is slowly born.

—On the other hand, in this case, some of the blame does lie with the party who originated the rumor: " ". After all, he has an account; he's been given his place to speak. Yet he says not a word and responds to no contact. Since he releases not so much as a byte of information, everything about him except that he's Japanese is a mystery. No one knows his face—and this is yet another factor that accelerates the growth of an urban legend.

—And so.

—It's time for an introduction.

This is it. The uncontested king of the global rankings for over 280 games. The legendary gamer who continues to make unbeatable records. " "—in the flesh—!

■■■

"……Ah…I'm gonna die; I'm gonna die… Ah, I died… Come on… Res me already!"

"…*Slurp*… I guess…it was too hard to use two mice with my feet…"

"What, just res me already— Hey, no fair, little sister! I haven't eaten anything in three days, and here you are leisurely slurping instant noodles—in the middle of a battle!"

"…Brother, you want some…? We've got some CalorieMate…"

"CalorieMate is for the bourgeois; who's gonna eat that? Just res me!"

"…*Sip*… Mm, sure."

Shvaa…pwing!

"Righto, props… Wait, what time is it?"

"…Uh…still, *eight o'clock in the middle of the night…*"

"Eight a.m. is the middle of the night? That's a new way of looking at it, my sister. What day is it?"

"…Dunno…it's my first, second—fourth, cup of noodles…so, I guess, fourth?"

"No, no, my sister, I didn't mean *the number of days we've been up.* I mean what day of what month?"

"…You…don't have a job… What does it matter?"

"It matters! There are events on online games and tournaments!"

—This young man and girl enjoying their online game spoke across the room without bothering with eye contact. The room was—probably big enough for sixteen tatami mats. Pretty big. But, with the countless consoles, four PCs each—eight total, along with the wiring that snaked around the floor with a modern art–like complexity, the opened game boxes, and the scattered noodle cups and plastic bottles they called "rations," there wasn't enough space left in the room to feel the original size. In the pale light of the LED displays they had chosen, like true gamers, for their fast refresh rate and the faint glimmer of the long-risen sun through the blackout curtains…they conversed.

"…Brother, aren't you gonna…get a job?"

"—Well, are *you* gonna go to school today?"

"…"

"…"

They spoke no further.

The brother: Sora ("Sky"/"Empty"). Eighteen, unemployed, virgin, unpopular, socially incompetent, video game vegetable. A young man with messy black hair, in jeans and a T-shirt, looking just the part of a shut-in. The sister: Shiro ("White"). Eleven, truant, friendless, bullied, socially phobic, video game vegetable. A girl who, with her pure white hair, looked far too unlike him to be related, hair which still dangled low and apparently uncared-for, covering her face as she sat in an elementary school sailor uniform she hadn't worn outside the house since she'd switched schools. The characters for their names put together spelled *Kuuhaku*: "Blank."

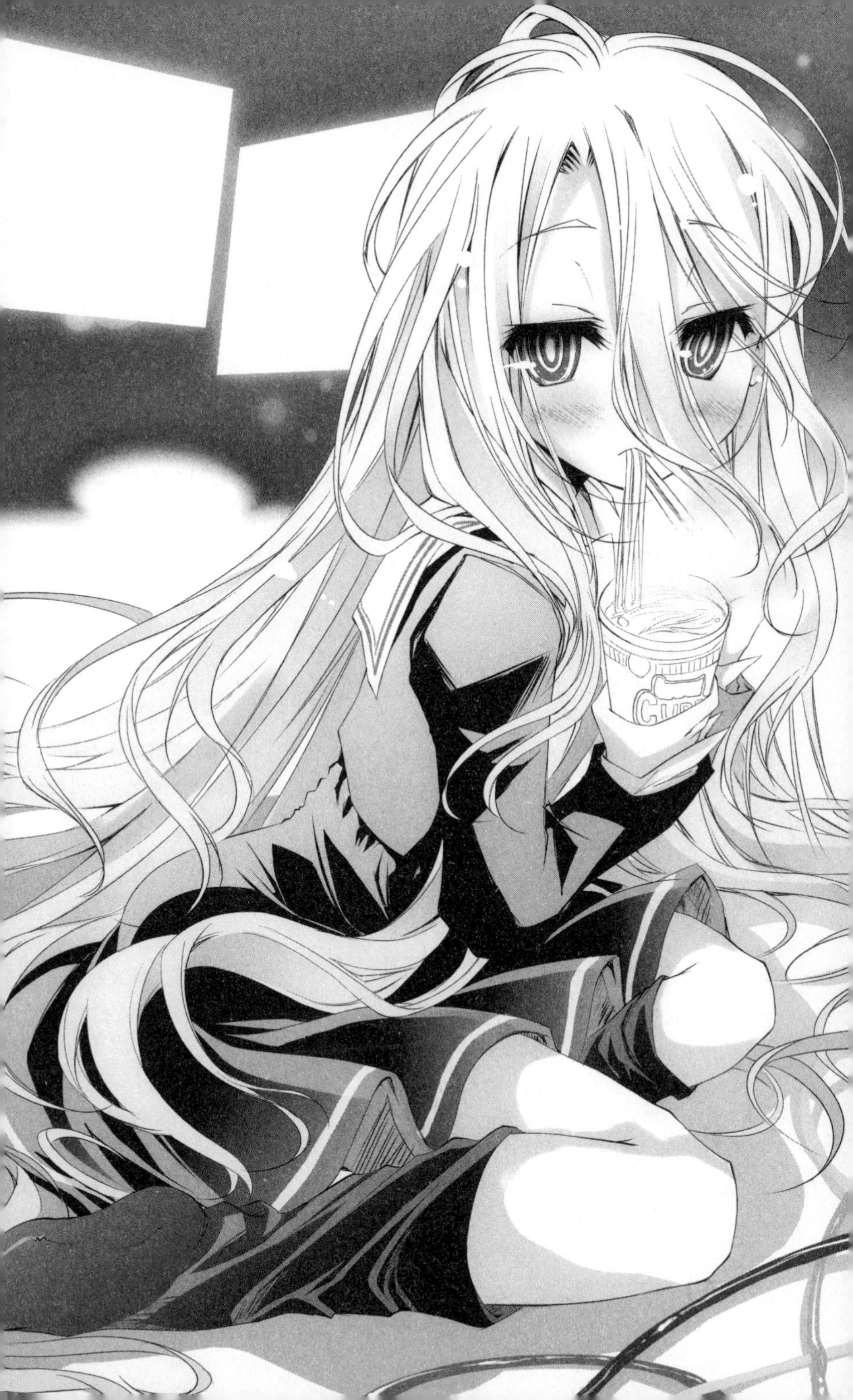

—Well. So, this is another kind of *urban legend*. You can leave it in the shadows. Or you can have your dreams.

■■■

—Very well, then: We see the processes by which *urban legends* form. In short, that they represent people's *wishes*, as explained earlier. For this world is chaos. Without fate and full only of coincidence. Unreasonable. Absurd. Devoid of meaning. And those who notice this but who don't want to admit it wish that the world could be just a little cooler. And this is what is born from that earnest wish: an *urban legend*.

—So, it's time. Let me make this uncool reality a little cooler for you. I offer you *a new urban legend*.

—And on that note, as a *convention*. As a *grace*.

—I'd like to open as follows:

—*Have you heard a rumor that goes like this?*—

They say that people who are just too good at games will one day get an e-mail. The body contains some cryptic words and a *URL* inviting them to a *certain game*. And, if you beat that game—

■■■

"…I'm pooped…gonna sleep."

"Hey, wait! If you go, who's gonna heal—"

"…You can do it, Brother."

"Well, theoretically, yes! If, in addition to the two characters I'm controlling with my hands, I control the two characters you abandoned with my feet!"

"……Hang in there."

"Wait—please, Shiro, I beg you! If you sleep now, everyone's gonna—or, well, *I'm* gonna die!——*Aaarrggghh*, damn it, fine, I'll show you!"

By now, the sister had stacked up five empty noodle cups. In other words, this was the fifth day the siblings' banter had continued without sleep. As the sister lay her head on a console to sleep, ignoring her brother's desperate, resigned cry, a sound entered her ear: *Bink*. It was the tablet telling her they'd gotten e-mail.

"Brother, mail."

"Your brother's busy playing four characters on four different screens. What do you expect him to do?!"

Manipulating four mice dexterously with both hands and both feet, this was all the brother could say as he whirled around the controls for a party of four like a lone dervish.

"I mean, it's probably just spam. Forget it!"

"…Maybe…it's from a friend?"

"—Of whose?"

"…Of…yours?"

"Ha-ha, that's a good one. I do believe my beloved sister just fired off a crack that cuts to my very core."

"…I hope…you get…why I didn't say 'of mine.'"

"Well, it's probably spam anyway. Wait, are you gonna sleep or not? If you're not gonna sleep, help meeeee! Ah, ah, I'm gonna die, I'm gonna die!"

The brother: Sora. To repeat—eighteen, unemployed, virgin, unpopular, socially incompetent, video game vegetable. Not that he was proud of it, but the idea that someone like him, who not only couldn't get a girlfriend but couldn't make a friend of any kind, could possibly have a "Friend" category in his list of e-mail senders was easily rejected. Evidently this applied to his sister, Shiro, as well.

"…Ughh… What a pain."

Still, Shiro mustered a consciousness that had been on the verge of sleep and rose. If it was just spam, then whatever. But if it was *spam for a new game*, well, that couldn't be missed.

"…Brother…where's the tablet?"

"Three o'clock, second pile, under the fourth porn game from the top—gahh, my feet are gonna cramp!"

Ignoring her brother's groans of suffering, Shiro followed his directions, fished through the pile—and found it. Perhaps you ask why a pair of shut-in losers would need a tablet? But that is a silly question. Of course—for games. On the other hand, there was another way that this pair was using said tablet. They had countless accounts and e-mail addresses for their countless games, so while reserving their PCs mostly for gaming, they had the tablet set to sync with over thirty e-mail accounts just so they could check their mail. You could call this "efficiency first." Or just "dumb."

"...The sound was *bink*... That's the notification for our third main address... This one, right?"

Displaying her monstrous memory, Shiro placidly dug through their e-mail. And—as, in the background, her brother let out a "whoop," apparently having managed to emerge victorious in a real-time battle while controlling four characters all by himself—she read the e-mail.

—One new message—Subject: Dear " ",

"......?"

The sister tilted her head. It wasn't especially unusual for " "—that is, Sora and Shiro—to receive e-mail. Requests for matches, requests for interviews, inflammatory challenges—there were plenty, but this...

"...Brother."

"Whatever could it be? My beloved, sick, twisted sister who just claimed she was going to sleep to force her brother to face a game all by himself, bound by physical restrictions, and who then didn't even go to sleep?"

"...This..."

As if she hadn't even heard her brother's sarcasm, she showed him the e-mail on the screen.

"Huh?—The hell's this?"

It seemed the brother also recognized there was something special about the e-mail.

"Save OK, drops OK..."

He made sure his progress was saved successfully and then closed the window for the first time in five days. He opened a mail client on the PC. And he squinted.

"How do they know Blank are a *brother and sister*?"

—Indeed, the brother knew that there were people online claiming " " was more than one person. But that wasn't the problem. The body just contained this one sentence with a URL:

> "Dear brother and sister, don't you ever feel you were born into the wrong world?"

"...The hell's this?"

"......"

The words were a little—no, *extremely*—creepy. And the URL was unfamiliar. There was no country code like ".jp" at the end. It was a URL of that sort that led to a specific page script—a direct link into a game.

"What do you...wanna do?"

The sister asked as if she didn't particularly care. But it was apparent that she, too, had taken an interest in this e-mail, whose sender seemed to know who they were. If she hadn't, she would've just put her head back on the console and slept. She left the decision to her brother—because she recognized it as *his area of expertise*, that is—

"Trying to play mind games? Oh well, it might be a bluff, but it might also be fun."

He ran security software to check for malware, then clicked the link. But...what appeared was unbelievably simple. An unadorned online chessboard.

"......*Yawn*...good night..."

"Hey, hey, wait. This is a challenge to Blank. If it's a high-level chess program, I can't beat it on my own."

The brother stopped the sister, who seemed to have immediately lost interest and was trying again to go to sleep.

"...Chess... Give me a break..."

"Yeah... I mean, I know how you feel..."

There was software that had shut out a grandmaster at the top of world chess: The sister had beaten it *twenty times in a row*. This was long ago. It wasn't surprising she'd lost interest in the game. But—

"Blank can't lose. At least stay up until we can see how good they are."

"…Ughh… Fine."

And so, Sora made his first move, then his second. Shiro watched disinterestedly. Actually, more just sleepily. She watched heavily as if she were rowing a boat. But then—after five or ten moves. Shiro's eyes, until then 80 percent closed, opened up and stared at the screen.

"…Huh? What's he…"

Just as Sora began to feel uneasy, Shiro stood up and spoke.

"…Brother, my turn…"

The brother handed over his seat obediently. This indicated that the sister had judged that the brother couldn't win. In other words, that the opponent *was worthy of playing the greatest chess player in the world.* The sister proceeded with her moves.

—Chess is a finite, zero-sum, two-player game with perfect information. It's a game with no room for luck to intervene. In theory, *an unbeatable strategy does exist,* but only in theory. Only if one can grasp all of the vast number of possible games: 10 to the 120th power. Practically speaking, such a thing is impossible.

—But Shiro says *it is not.* She says with conviction that *all you have to do is read all 10-to-the-120th-power possibilities.* And she did in fact beat the world's top chess program twenty times in a row. In chess, the person who goes first merely has to pick the best move to win, and the person who goes second can only draw. That's the theory, anyway. She played this game against a program that explored two hundred million possibilities a second. *She won twenty times in a row, alternating who moved first,* just to demonstrate the imperfection of the program. And yet.

"…No way."

She opened her eyes in surprise.

—Meanwhile, however, her brother was noticing something strange about the way things were going.

"Calm down. The player's human, is the thing."

"—Huh?"

"A program always makes the best move. It has unlimited concentration, but it can only move according to established strategies. That's why you can win. But—this guy."

The brother pointed to the screen.

"He's making a bad move on purpose to lure you in. You assumed that it was the *program's* mistake. That was *your mistake.*"

"……Nghh."

The sister had no counterargument for her brother.

—It was true that, in chess…no, in almost any game…her technical skill vastly outmatched his. Truly: a genius gamer. However, in *mind games, reading the opponent, and manipulation,* in all kinds of insight into that wild card of the opponent's emotions—the brother's skills were superhuman. This was why " "—the combination of Sora and Shiro—was *unbeaten.*

"Don't worry. Just calm down. If the opponent's not a program, then there's even less chance you could lose. Just don't let him rattle you. I'll explain his traps and strategies, so cool it."

"…Okay… I'll try."

This was it. The mechanism behind a single gamer running away with the top global ranking for so many games.

————…

This game, played without time control, extended over six hours. The adrenaline and dopamine secreted by their brains made them forget they'd been up for five days straight, swept away their fatigue, and pulled their concentration up to its limits. Six hours—yet the battle felt as if it actually took days. Finally, the decisive moment came. The emotionless voice echoing from the speaker.

"Checkmate."

The siblings—won.

""————""

After a long silence…

""*Hhffffff………*""

They exhaled all their breath. It spoke to a match such as to make them forget to breathe. When they were finally done, they laughed.

"…Wow… It's been so long…since I played a game this hard…"

"Ha-ha, it's the first time I've even seen you think a game was hard."

"...Wow... Brother, is the opponent...really human?"

"Yeah, there's no mistaking it. I could see him hesitating when you didn't take his bait, getting slightly confused when the traps he'd laid didn't go off. It's a human for sure—either that or a monster."

"...I wonder what he's like."

The sister, who had shut out a program that had shut out the grandmasters, was becoming interested in an opponent.

"Well, it could actually be a grandmaster? Programs are precise, but people are complex."

"...I see... In that case... Next, I wanna...play shogi, with the Ryu-oh..."

"I wonder if the Ryu-oh is open to playing online. Well, we'll give it some thought!"

As they conversed, grinning with the feeling of satisfaction produced by endorphins after a match, it happened again.

—*Bink!* The sound of another e-mail notification.

"Must be our opponent just now? Come on, open it up."

"...Okay, okay."

And—as for the e-mail's contents? Just this:

> "Marvelous. With skills like that, *surely you must find it hard to live in this world*?"

All it took was one line. Their psyches flash-froze. The pair had just weathered a raging battle on the LED display. From behind them shone artificial light. The hum of the fans of computers and game equipment. Countless wires wriggling across the floor. Scattered trash. Clothes strewn everywhere. A space hidden from the sense of time, walled by the curtains that blocked out the sun. *Isolated from the world*—sixteen tatami mats' worth of cramped space. That was their world—all of it.

—Bitter memories rushed through their minds. The brother who had been born no good and who was therefore too good at reading people's words and motives. The sister who had been born too smart, and because of that and her pure white hair and red eyes, had no one who understood her. The siblings who had been abandoned, even by their parents, then left alone in this world and who finally closed their hearts to a past that not even the most generous interpretation could recall as happy—no, to a *present as well.* The sister looked down in silence. The brother pounded his anger onto the keyboard at the one who had made his sister look down.

"Thanks for your goddamn concern. Who the hell are you?"

The reply came almost immediately.

—Or was it even a reply? An e-mail ignoring the question came.

"What do you think of this world? Is it fun? Is it easy to live in?"

Reading this, he forgot even to be angry and met eyes with his sister. There was nothing they needed to confirm. They knew the answer.

—That it was the most fail kind of game ever.

…A stupid game with no clear rules or goal. Seven billion players all taking their turns whenever they wanted. Penalized if you won too much. —The sister who, thanks to being too smart, was alone and bullied with no one to understand her. Penalized if you lost too much. —The brother who kept failing and getting yelled at by his teachers and parents, yet kept smiling. No right to pass. The bullying only got worse if she was silent. If she spoke too much, she'd be hated for crossing a line. And *he'd* be hated for seeing through to people's true motives. There was no way to tell the goal, read the stats, or even identify the genre. Even if you followed the rules that were laid out, you'd be punished—and worst of all: *those who just ignored the rules stood at the top*—. Compared to this awful life, any other game was just too easy.

"*Tsk*—asshole."

Sora patted the head of his young sister who was still looking down.

—The pair who had just displayed a godlike performance were

nowhere to be found. The two that were left were downcast—downtrodden—some of the lowest weaklings in society. Nowhere to go, cast out by the world—nothing more. The irritation brought the fatigue back in a rush. As the brother moved the cursor to the Start button to turn off the computer for the first time in a while, he heard: *Bink!*—another e-mail notification entering his ear. His hand proceeded to Shut Down regardless.

—But his sister stopped him.

> "What if there was a *world where every-*
> *thing was decided by simple games*—"

The two read this suspiciously, but with imagination and longing they couldn't conceal.

> "What if there was a *world on a board* where
> the goal and rules were clear? What would
> you think?"

They looked back at each other, grinned in self-deprecation, and nodded. The brother put his hands on the keyboard. *So that's where he was going with this.*

> "Yeah, if there's a world like that, *we*
> *really* were *born in the wrong one.*"

—He echoed the words of the initial e-mail. And hit Send.

—For a moment.

Faint static rippled across the computer screen. At the same time, everything in the room halted with a thump, as if the breaker had been tripped. All except for one thing—the screen that showed the e-mail. And—

"Wha-what?!"

"…?"

There was a sound as if the house was creaking, a sound like the crackle of electricity. The brother looked around in a panic as the sister spaced out, clueless as what to what was happening. The static grew inexorably stronger and finally took over like the snow on an untuned TV. And then from the speakers—no. Unmistakably *from the screen*. This time it wasn't text—*a voice* came back.

"I agree. You certainly were born in the wrong world."

Not only the screen, but now the whole room was taken over by the static. Suddenly, white arms extended from the screen's surface.

"Wha—?!"

"…Ee—"

The limbs reached out from the screen and grabbed the siblings' arms. They were pulled in with a force that was too strong to fight. *Into the screen—*.

"Then I'll *let you be born again—into the world you should have been!*"

—…And then—.

Everything turned white. It was because he'd opened his eyes—it was the light of the sun. He knew this by a burning sensation on his retinas that he hadn't felt in a long time. Finally, the brother realized something from the sight that entered his pupils as they started to adjust to the light. He was—in the sky.

"*Wwaaaah?!*"

His cramped little room had become, all of a sudden, a wide and sweeping vista.

—But his scream was not because of the *strangeness of the landscape* that entered his eyes. Sora's brain was accelerating to grasp the situation, almost enough to fry his mental circuits, and that was why he was screaming.

"What… what the hell?!"

—No matter how you looked at it, no matter how many times. There in the sky was a *floating island*. And no matter how many times he second-guessed his eyes and head, out at the limits of his vision, flying through the sky, was a *dragon*. The giant chess pieces visible deep in the mountains beyond the horizon were huge enough to confuse his sense of perspective. It belonged in a game—a *fantasy landscape*.

This was clearly not a landscape from the Earth he knew. But more importantly—*most* importantly—from the clouds sweeping out under his eyes, he realized that the feeling of weightlessness *was because he was falling.* That they were unmistakably in the middle of a skydive with no parachute. Taking all this in and turning his shriek to—

"Oh, I'm about to die."

—levels of conviction took the brother all of three seconds. But then his tragic conviction was broken through by a voice ringing out resoundingly beside him.

"Welcome to my world!"

Before the grand and strange landscape, a falling *boy* spread his arms wide and beamed.

"This is the utopia you've dreamed of, Disboard, the 'world on a board'! *A world where everything is decided by simple games!* That's right—*even people's lives and countries' borders!*"

She was maybe ten seconds behind Sora. Shiro, seeming to have finally grasped the situation, opened her eyes wide and grabbed on to her brother, looking as if about to cry.

"Wh-wh-who—are you—?"

Shiro raised a cry of protest with all her strength, yet as if whispering. But the *boy* went on smiling happily and said:

"Me? Well, I live over there."

As he said it, he pointed to a giant chess piece beyond the horizon such as Sora had seen.

"I suppose if I were to put it in the terms of your world—I'm *God,* I guess!"

The self-proclaimed God said this with deliberate cuteness, sticking his index finger to his cheek.

But what difference did it make now?

"Whatever. Hey, what are we supposed to do?! The ground's coming—*aghhhh, Shiro!*"

"…~~~~~!"

Drawing Shiro's hands into his chest, Sora put himself beneath her, though the gesture was questionably meaningful. Shiro shrieked into Sora's body with a muted cry. Meanwhile, the boy who claimed to be a god told them jauntily:

"I hope to see you again. Probably not too long in the future."

—With that, the pair's consciousness faded.

————…

"*Ugh…ughhh…*"

The feeling of soil. The scent of flowers—when he came to, Sora was lying on the ground. He groaned and got up.

"—Wha-what just happened…?"

—A dream? Sora thought so but didn't say it.

"…*Ughh*…what a weird dream."

Sora's sister woke up after him and groaned.

—*Aw, Sister. After I made a point of not saying it, too. You didn't have to go and set the "It wasn't a dream" flag.* With these thoughts, he stood up, and no matter how he tried to pretend he didn't notice, there was *soil under his feet.* An unfamiliar sky soared overhead, and—

"*Gaaaah!*"

Sora realized that he was standing at the edge of a cliff and stepped back in a panic.

—Looking over the panorama from the cliff, he saw an unbelievable landscape spreading out before them.

…No, that's not it. Let me rephrase that. There was an island in the sky. A dragon. And giant chess pieces beyond the mountains on the horizon. So it was the same weird landscape they had seen while falling. So it—wasn't a dream.

"Hey, little sister."

"…Hnh?"

The siblings spoke as they looked out with vacant eyes.

"I've often thought that life was an impossible game, a game for masochists. But this…"

"…Yeah…"

They spoke in unison.

""It's finally glitched out… What…the hell? This game is *epic fail*…""

And then they lost consciousness once more.

■■■

—Have you heard a rumor that goes like this?—

They say that people who are just too good at games will one day get an e-mail. The body contains just a few words and a URL. And, if you click the link, a certain game———will start. If you beat the game, they say *you disappear from this world*. And then—

There's an *urban legend* that says you'll be invited to *another* world.

...Do you believe it?

⏻ CHAPTER 1
BEGINNER

—Once upon a time, there was a time still longer ago. When the Old Deus race fought with their relations and creations for the title of One True God. With that, the battle continued so long as to make one faint. There was no ground not stained by blood, no sky not filled by screams. All thinking things hated each other, and to destroy their enemies they murdered and slaughtered without mercy. Elves mobilized from their little villages, honing their magic, hunting their foes. Dragonias followed their instincts, giving themselves over to butchery, and Werebeasts devoured their prey like animals. The earth was laid to waste and swallowed in dusk, and yet still fell deeper into the darkness of the war of the gods. The "Devil" emerged as a mutation of the Phantasma, and monsters of the Devil's breed swarmed across the land. In this world, royal houses, their many beauties, and most of all, their heroes—these did not exist. Immanity was of no consequence. The people built nations, formed cabals, staking everything *merely to survive*. There are still no heroic tales for the bard to sing—so blood-drenched was this time, long before this land and sea and sky came to be called *Disboard*. But, even upon this chaos of war that was thought to be never-ending, the curtain dropped. The land, the sea, the sky—the planet itself. Everything was haggard, worn-out, exhausted, and the struggle toward mutual destruction could not be sustained any further. And, thus—the deity who had the most strength left came to sit upon the throne of the One True God. A god who *had never once intervened in the war.* A god who had stayed an observer.

This deity who sat on the throne of the One True God looked around at the state of the world. And he spoke to all things that wandered its surface.

—O ye who expend your might and force and arms and mortality building a tower of the dead, *and yet call yourselves wise*, prove me this: What shall set you apart from the witless beasts?

Every race spoke up to prove its own wisdom. But every word rang hollow before the wasted world. In the end, not a creature could give the God a response that answered. The God spoke.

—On this heaven and earth, all bodily injury and plunder shall be forbidden.

His words became a covenant, an absolute and immutable *rule of the world.* And, thus, from that day, *combat* vanished from the world. But each of the thinking things spoke up to the God: that, though combat vanished, *conflict* remained. And so the God said, very well.

—O sixteen seeds that claim yourselves wise, ye Ixseeds:
expend ye your *reason and wit and talent and wealth*,
building a tower of wisdom to prove yourselves wise.

The God drew out sixteen playing pieces—and smiled mischievously. And thus were born the *Ten Covenants*, and thus ended the world of *war.* So it came to pass that all quarrels should be settled by *games.*

The new One True God had a name—Tet. He who was once known as the *God of Play...*

■■■

On the continent of Lucia, in the Kingdom of Elkia—the capital, Elkia. The continent that swept northeast with the Equator at its south, and there was a small city in a small country at the western tip. No trace was left of the age of myth, when the kingdom had reigned over half the continent. Now, all that was left was one last city—the capital, a tiny city-state.

—To be more exact: It was the last bastion of Immanity.

In the city, just beyond the downtown area, in the suburbs, was a single building that housed a tavern and an inn of just the sort that might show up in an RPG. Two girls sat on opposite sides of a table, surrounded by spectators, playing a game. One was a redhead who looked to be in her midteens, her manner and accoutrement suggesting high breeding. And the other—. She was probably about the same age as the redhead, though her mien and attire suggested someone quite a bit older. This black-haired girl was wrapped in a black veil and cape as if for a funeral. The game they were playing... appeared to be poker. Their expressions contrasted sharply: The redhead was a mask of seriousness, perhaps from tension. Meanwhile, the black-haired girl seemed unconcerned, with a dead, expressionless face. The reason was clear to see—piled high in front of the black-haired girl and low in front of the redhead: *coins*. The obvious interpretation was that the redhead was losing hopelessly.

"...Can you hurry up?"

"Qu-quiet, you. I'm thinking, don't you see!"

—In the tavern, the crowd jeered crudely, already intoxicated despite the early hour. The redhead's brow knit further in frustration. In any case it seemed that some excitement was being had.

......——.Outside the tavern where the game was being held, a young girl wearing a hood sat at a table on the terrace and peered in through the window.

"...Some excitement... What's this?"

"Huh? Don't you know? Are you folks from another country—wait, there are no more other human countries."

At the table next to the girl peering through the window sat another pair, who sat around a table playing a game. A young man wearing a hood like the young girl's, and a middle-aged man with facial hair and a beer belly. The young man answered.

"Oh, you know… We came from way out in the sticks. We don't really know much about what's been going on in the city."

As it happened, the game they were playing was the same as the one inside…*poker*—but here they were using bottle caps.

The middle-aged man replied dubiously to the youth. "You're saying there is countryside left in the territory Immanity still owns…? You must be some kind of hermit."

"Ha-ha, something like that. So, what's all this about?"

The youth dodged the topic and drew an answer from the fuzzy man.

"Right now, Elkia is having a grand gambling tournament to decide the next monarch."

While still watching what was happening inside, the hooded girl questioned further. "…To decide the next…monarch?"

"Indeed. According to the will of the late king."

«The crown of the next monarch we bequeath not upon our royal bloodline, but upon *the greatest gambler among humans*.»

The fuzzy man spoke on while stacking his bottle caps.

"You know, Immanity lost everything in the play for dominion, and now all that's left is Elkia, and Elkia has nothing left but her capital—so it's too late to worry about appearances."

"Hmm, *play for dominion, eh?* Interesting stuff you've got going on here."

So said the hooded young man. Following the hooded girl's lead, the young man took an interest in the proceedings in the tavern, peering in.

"—So, what, are those girls eligible to be the future queen?"

"—Hmmm? I'm not sure 'eligible' is the right word. Anyone of Immanity may enter. But—" he added as he turned his gaze into the tavern.

—They were playing poker. Didn't she know the term "poker

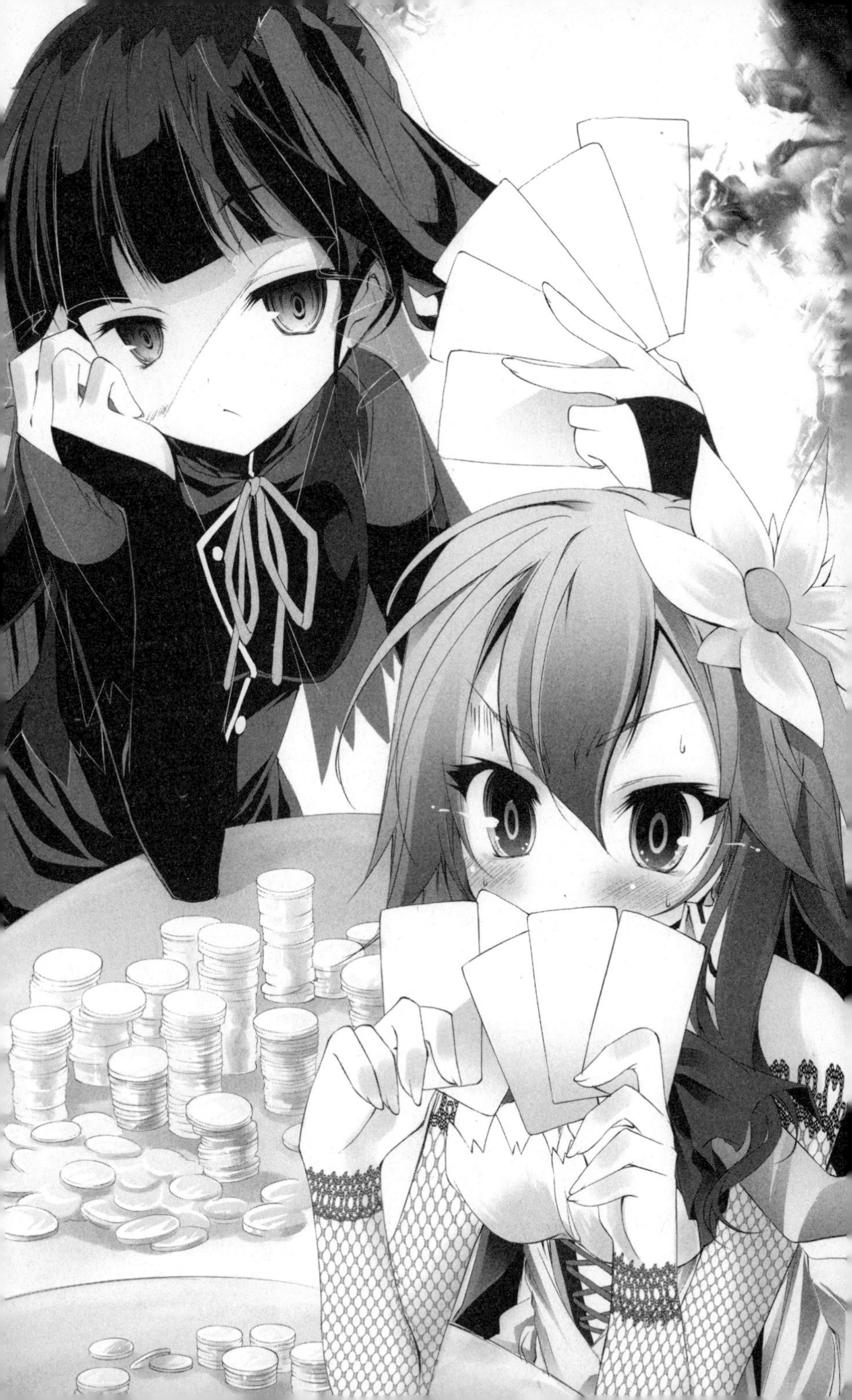

face"? With a glance at the redhead, who was glaring at her hand as if she would groan audibly any second, the man spoke.

"The redhead is Stephanie Dola—she's part of the bloodline of the former king. The way the will is written, if someone not of royal blood takes the crown, she'll lose everything, so she's aiming to put herself on the throne.

"After that king brought us humans to such ruin, that his family should struggle so hard…" The man added this and sighed. It was a blunt explanation of the excitement inside.

"Hm…mm…"

"Hmm… 'Play for dominion'—*even national borders are decided by games*, huh?"

The hooded girl and young man muttered their thoughts to each other. The girl impressed. The young man amused.

"So, that's how it is: it's a free-for-all gambling tournament."

"…*Free-for-all?*"

"Basically, any member of Immanity who wishes to stand for the crown may speak up and challenge his rivals to a game, by any means he sees fit. He who loses shall be stripped of his right, and he who stands left at the end shall be king."

—Well, well, these rules were easy enough to understand. Excellent. Still, the hooded young man asked doubtfully:

"…Sounds pretty casual. Is that really going to work?"

"It is, after all, a play for dominion under the *Ten Covenants*, which promise that each may wager whatever each agrees is of equal value, playing according to any rules—anyone may contest anyone at anything at any time."

"…No, well, that's not exactly what I meant."

As the hooded young man muttered suggestively, he peered once more into the tavern. "…No wonder she's losing," the girl muttered to him.

"Yeah, no kidding."

As the two conversed, the young man drew a rectangular object from his pocket. He faced it toward the inside of the tavern and manipulated something, and there was a sound: *snap*.

—And the middle-aged man grinned.

"So, lad? Should you really be worrying about other people's battles?" With that, the man opened his hand flat. "Full house. Sorry about that."

Sure of his victory and thinking of *what would come after*, the man's lips curled in a filthy smile.

—But the hooded youth replied as if never interested from the start, as if he'd just now remembered that he was playing a game of poker. "Huh? Ohh, yeah, sorry, that's right."

As the youth carelessly opened his hand, the middle-aged man's eyes opened wide.

"A r-*royal flush*?!"

The youth had been holding the strongest hand in the game without so much as a peep. The man stood up and shouted.

"*Y-you*…you think you can pull one over on me?!"

"Whaa… Come on, don't be rude… What basis do you have for saying that?"

The youth blithely slid out his chair and stood up. The man pressed further.

"The odds of a royal flush are one in 650,000! How could that happen?"

"It just happened to be that one in 650,000 today. Bad luck, old man."

The youth slipped out the words and held out his hand.

"Now, may I accept the promised wager?"

"——Damn it!"

Clucking, the man held out his purse, and then another pouch.

"The Sixth of the *Ten Covenants*: '*Wagers sworn by the Covenants are absolutely binding*'—fine, good game."

"…Thanks…Pops."

As the hooded young man calmly left his chair, and the girl nodded her head and chased after him, the bearded man watched them go into the tavern, and an apparent friend of his approached him.

"Ho, I was watching the whole time, but did you really bet everything you had on you?"

"Aahh… Mercy me, how will I pay the bills…"

"But, wait, back up. You bet the money you needed for your bills? What the hell kind of wager did your opponent make?"

The fuzzy man sighed and answered with a look of disinterest.

"That *I could do whatever I wanted with them.*"

"Wha—"

"I did think it sounded too good to be true…but they seemed unworldly, and I thought it might… What?"

"No, I mean…which are you?"

"—Come again?"

"I mean…*a fruit or a pedo*? Either one is…well…"

"Wha—h-hey, wait!"

"Oh, relax; I won't tell your wife. Just buy me a meal!"

"It's—it's not like that! And, anyway, I just lost all the money I had! And, to begin with—"

——……

"…Brother…that's not fair."

"Huh? What's *your* problem?"

"…You intentionally…cheated, in such an obvious way."

—Yes, just as the man had said. A royal flush was a hand that *could hardly ever happen.* Laying out a hand like that was tantamount to declaring that you had cheated. But—

"The Eighth of the *Ten Covenants*—'If cheating is discovered in a game, it shall be counted as a loss—'"

The young man mumbled the rules of this world he had just learned as if to confirm them.

"—In other words, as long as it's not discovered, you can cheat. Isn't it great we confirmed this?"

Suggesting that he was just trying it out as a casual experiment, he stretched.

"Welp, now we've got some war funds."

"…Brother… Do you understand the money here?"

"How am I supposed to understand it? But don't worry; this is what your brother does best."

They talked so as not to be heard by the bearded man and his apparent friend. Then they entered the tavern-inn.

■■■

Ignoring the table at the center where the crowd still hooted over the match, they approached the counter. The hooded young man dropped the pouch and purse with a thud on the counter and asked slowly:

"So. Two people, one room, one bed is fine. How many nights can we stay?"

A man who appeared to be the master. A glance. A moment's hesitation, and then:

"…That'll be one night, with board."

But the hooded young man responded coyly—*smiling, except with his eyes.*

"Aha-haa… Look here, Mister, we've been awake for five days, and we're dead on our feet from walking way more than usual. We're exhausted, you know? Can you just cut to the chase and tell us *how many nights, really*?"

"—What?"

"I mean, if you want to try to swindle people you think are just bumpkins who don't know the value of money here, that's up to you, but let me just give you a tip—when you're lying, you should *watch the direction you look and the tone of your voice*, okay?"

—Sharpening his gaze to see through everything, the young man spoke with a smile. With a line of cold sweat and a cluck, the master answered:

"*Tsk.* It's two nights."

"And there you go again… Well, let's split the difference and say ten nights with three meals."

"What! What difference are you splitting?! Fine—fine—three nights with board. It's true!"

"Oh, is that so? Then give us a discount and make it five nights with board."

"Wha—"

"Come on, you can treat us with some of that money you're embezzling as you rip off customers, right?"

"Wha—wait—how—"

"You're the *master of the tavern, not the inn, right*? I'll be happy to rat you out."

The young man smiled wanly, but played dirty. The master strained his face and answered.

"You've got an innocent face, but a dirty disposition, kid... Fine, four nights with three meals; how's that?"

"Great; it's been a pleasure."

The young man smiled and took the room key.

"You go up to the third floor, all the way back, and it's on your left. *Hff...* What's your name?"

Looking in a sour mood, the master took out the register. The hooded young man answered.

"Hmm... Just leave it blank."

Sora spun the key he'd received around his finger. He thumped his hand onto the back of his sister, who was watching the table where all the match excitement was happening.

"Hey, I got four nights. Sing praises upon your brother and his— what's up?"

Shiro was staring at Stepha...whatever her name was, the redhead that the bearded man had been talking about. She was still suffering, and still showing it clearly on her face, so much so that it was hard to imagine she might still think she could win.

"...That one's—gonna lose."

"Well, yeah. So?"

If she showed her emotions on her face so obviously, there was no way she could win regardless of her draw. Perhaps the bearded man was right when he suggested that the blood of the royal family was stupid. As Sora pondered this—he realized.

"—Oh—"

He realized the true meaning of his sister's words and opened his mouth.

"Aagh, I get it... That's scary..."

"...Mm."

Sora murmured and Shiro nodded, looking at the black-haired girl.

"Now, that's... *This world's cheats* are amazing. I don't wanna go up against that..."

"...They put you to shame, brother..."

Sora, apparently irked by these words, argued defensively. "Hng, don't be stupid. It's not how great your cheats are; it's how you use them."

"...Brother, can you beat that?"

"—Guess this really is a fantasy world... It doesn't quite click; I mean, it kind of feels too natural... Maybe I really have played too many games?"

Not bothering to answer his sister's question, Sora was already walking up to the third floor.

"......Dumb question...never mind."

This was Shiro's apology.

——That's right: For " ", *loss* was inconceivable.

And...on their way, as they passed Ste...what's-her-name, the redhead, on a whim Sora whispered. "...Ma'am, you know you're being hoodwinked, right?"

"——Huh?"

She was stunned. Her blue eyes went round, contrasting with her red hair. Having had their say, Sora and Shiro went up to the third floor, feeling the dumbfounded gaze of the girl on their backs... Even so, they left it at that, proceeding to their room without looking back.

■■■

Turning the key, hearing the creaking of the shaky fittings, they looked beyond the opened door. The room inside—was a cheap-looking wooden room like ones they'd seen in *Obl*vion* and *Skyr*m*. The floor squeaked with footsteps, and the room was small. In the corner was a sad excuse for a table with seating. Otherwise, there was a bed and a window. That summed up this most basic of interiors.

They entered the room, locked the door, and finally took off their hoods.

The young man in just a T-shirt with jeans and sneakers, with messy black hair—Sora. The small girl in a sailor suit with red eyes hidden by long, frizzy, pure white hair—Shiro. Throwing off the robe he'd borrowed so as not to stand out (his appearance being rather unfamiliar to this world), Sora flopped down on the lone bed as if deeply relieved. He took his phone out of his pocket—and put a *check mark in his task scheduler.*

"*Objective*: Find lodging… *Achieved.*—That's that. I can say it now, right?"

"…Mm. I think so."

After checking the item off, he uttered from the very bottom his heart a single statement: "Aaaahh, so tiiiiiiiiiiiiiiiiiirred……"

And how. He'd sworn he wouldn't say it until that moment, but now that he'd said the words and the dam was broken, Sora's grousing started flooding out unstoppably.

"I can't believe this shit! Not only did we actually have to go outside, we had to walk, like, forever!"

Shiro followed his lead in finally taking off her robe, and she patted out the wrinkles on her sailor suit. She opened the window and looked out. From the open window, she could just see the cliff where they had been—far in the distance.

"…People can accomplish great things, when they want to."

"Yeah, *you can't do anything if you don't feel like it*—that's a great way of expressing our reality."

This was a rather negative interpretation—but his sister nodded in assent.

"But, man, I totally thought my legs had atrophied by now. I'm surprised I could walk that far."

"…'Cause you were using mice with your feet?"

"Ohh, yeah! It's really true that skills are transferable!"

"…Never thought they'd be…transferred, this way."

Their comedy routine seemed to be approaching its limits. Shiro's eyes started to close more than halfway. The sister wobbled dizzily down onto the bed onto which Sora had collapsed. She didn't express it on her face, but the pain of her fatigue was clear from her breathing.

—Well, that was hardly surprising. She may have been a genius girl, but she was still a lass of only eleven. After five days without sleep, she'd played the chess match and gone on a lengthy forced march interrupted only by spots of unconsciousness—she'd traveled a distance even Sora found grueling (albeit on Sora's back toward the end) without a word of complaint, and that much was worthy of wonder. For that reason itself, Sora had sworn to himself he wouldn't complain until now.

"Good job. You're such a good little girl, my sister; your brother's very proud of you."

He stroked her hair as if to comb it.

"......Mm. We got a place...to sleep."

"Yeah, when we were attacked by those bandits, I really didn't know what would happen."

Sora thought back to a few hours earlier. In other words...when they first found themselves stranded in this world.

■■■

"—Well, then, what shall we do?"

Sora spoke, and Shiro shook her head. They'd come back from their second spell of unconsciousness. Sora had shouted and ranted about the absurdity of life. Shiro had spaced fully out, sigh after sigh escaping her lips. Seeming to finally grow weary of this, they regained their composure in the midst of their fatigue. They moved away from the cliff and sat down beside a simple road that hadn't even been paved.

"...Brother, why here?"

"You know, in RPGs, they always have these big roads? Where people pass by..."

It was questionable how far his knowledge from games would apply. But anyway.

"—So, this is where we check what we have."

Sora had a feeling that was always what they did in survival stories. With only that wisdom, they took out their items from their pockets one after another. What came out: Two smartphones (Sora's and Shiro's). Two DSP handheld game consoles. Two modular spare batteries, two solar chargers, two multicharger cables. And the tablet Shiro had ended up carrying along with her—

…It was a wealth of equipment not at all befitting castaways. However, it was all for games. They carried it with them at all times, in the bathroom, in the bath, such that even in a blackout they'd never be without games.

Though truth be told, it was questionable whether this kind of wealth would help in a real survival scenario.

"…I guess there wouldn't be any signal in a fantasy world."

Sora looked at his phone. It said there was no service.

—On the other hand, the backlight would serve as a flashlight at night, and it could take photos and videos. Maps obviously didn't work, but he could use it as a compass. Feeling gratitude for the sophistication of modern phones, Sora spoke.

"…All right, let's turn off your phone and the tablet and charge them up with the solar charger while the sun is out. I have a bunch of e-books on the tablet I downloaded to study for quiz games; in the worst-case scenario, we might need a survival manual."

"…Roger."

She obediently turned them off and connected them to the solar charger. Shiro had learned from experience that it was best to follow her brother's instructions when in an unforeseen situation.

…So: It was possible to use the power of science (Sora's phone) to find which way was north. But, still, it was just as if they had been cast out on the wide blue sea with no maps and only a compass. With the fruits of cutting-edge technology in hand, they sat on the wayside, lost in life.

"—Hey?"

There were a few people walking down the road.

"Hey! Sweet! It's time for my RPG experience to shine!"

"…Brother, they look…weird."

And the group that had shown up suddenly picked up speed and spread to surround them. Their green garb, their shoes that looked easy to run in—

"Oh, God, they're bandits."

Sora looked up at the sky and said this without thinking. That the very first people they should encounter on the road should be *Hello, we are bandits from a fantasy world.* Just as if straight from a template, this mean-looking bunch—Sora was just about ready to curse the heavens in earnest. Feeling danger to their persons, Sora physically guarded Shiro.

—But what the bandits said.

"Heh-heh…If you want to pass—play a game with us."

"……The siblings could only look at each other—but.

"—Oh, yeah, that kid said that *everything's decided by games in this world.*"

"This is what bandits are like here?"

They immediately got the picture: Compared to robbers in *their own world*…this looked so heartwarming, so cute, even, that they couldn't help but laugh.

"What are you sniggerin' about, you whelps! If you don't play our game, you ain't goin' a step further!" the bandits shouted, not comprehending why they were being laughed at. Regardless, the siblings conspired with each other in voices just too low for the bandits to hear.

"So, they gang up on one person, cheat, and take everything they have—yeah?"

"…Sounds…perfect."

Having talked it over, Sora clapped his hands twice.

"Okay, that's fine; we'll play you. But I regret to inform you we haven't got shit."

"Hrmm, no matter, lad; we'll just—"

But Sora went on, interrupting the bandit.

"*If we lose, do anything you want with us.* Sell us off somewhere, whatever."

"—Huh?"

The bandit squinted at this proposal stealing a march on what he was going to say.

"In exchange, if we win—"

With a spine-chilling smile across his face—the brother continued.

"—show us the way to the nearest city! Oh, and give us the robes those two are wearing. I mean, you know how the people from another world always stand out with their weird clothes. Oh, and tell us all about this world's game rules!"

Showing the adaptability of his brain to all games, he rattled off requests as if he already knew he would win.

■■■

Bringing his thoughts back to the present, Sora murmured.

"*Ten Covenants*—hmm. Shiro, have you got them down?"

"…Mm. Interesting…rules."

His sister answered drowsily as if about to fall asleep. Once they'd been soundly beaten, the bandits had explained the *rules of this world*. He took out his phone, where he had jotted them down, and read them over.

The Ten Covenants—. Apparently they were absolute rules set by the God of this world. The sister had memorized them easily, it seemed, but what the brother had on his phone was this:

1. In this world, all bodily injury, war, and plunder is forbidden.
2. All conflicts shall be settled by victory and defeat in games.
3. Games shall be played for wagers that each agrees are of equal value.
4. Insofar as it does not conflict with "3," any game or wager is permitted.

5. The party challenged shall have the right to determine the game.
6. Wagers sworn by the Covenants are absolutely binding.
7. For conflicts between groups, an agent plenipotentiary shall be established.
8. If cheating is discovered in a game, it shall be counted as a loss.
9. The above shall be absolute and immutable rules, in the name of the God.

"And Ten—'*Let's all have fun together*'..."

—...

"It sounds like it's ending with 'The above' at Nine, but then there's Ten..."

It seemed as if it were saying that having fun together was not mandatory. Or maybe it was something more like: *Not that I think you bozos are capable of having fun together.* These ironic "rules" recalled the face of the "God" or whatever, who looked like *he* was having fun, at least.

"That kid who pulled us into this world—if that's 'God,' He's not a bad guy."

The brother put away his phone and smirked to himself. As he lay on the bed and thought...it seemed that the fatigue finally caught up to him, as his consciousness clouded and his thoughts began to diffuse.

"...Guess it's only natural when you think about it. After staying up for five days, suddenly there's this..."

Beside the mumbling brother, his sister held on to his arm, her breath already indicating that she was asleep. When she lay down and her bangs fell from her face, it revealed skin white as porcelain, a face composed like a work of art. It seemed like a bad joke that they were siblings. She was like a doll.

"—I'm always telling you you should at least put on a blanket... You'll catch a cold."

"...Mm."

To the *brother* who spoke to her, the *sister* asked for a blanket with her vacant response. He hesitated to put the dusty-smelling blanket over his sister, but it was probably better than nothing. Watching the sleeping face of his sister as he heard the sound of her breath, the brother thought:

—*Now, what are we gonna do after this...*

So Sora took out his phone and started fiddling with it. He looked to see if he had any apps that might be of use, and then it occurred to him:

—*In stories about people drifting between worlds, they always worry first about how to get home...*

—His parents were already gone.

—His sister wasn't *accepted by society.*

—He himself could never *accept society.*

—*In that world*, there was no place for him except in the screen.

"...Hey. Why is it that, when the main character gets thrown into another world, they always try to go back to their *own* world?"

Knowing she was asleep, he went and tossed out the question anyway, but, as expected, there was no answer. After their four nights here, what should they do next? He gave a shot at thinking about it—but, before he could reach a conclusion, sleep shut off his train of thought.

■■■

—*Knock, knock.* The gentle knock at the door was enough to wake him—probably the jumpy nerves from arriving in this unfamiliar land. Shushing his body's screaming that it needed more sleep, Sora's brain spun up rapidly.

"......Mnng..."

—This did not, however, seem to apply to his sister. She was still clutching her brother's right arm, deep in sleep, dripping drool. This comforted him like nothing else; every bit the enviable young girl in the midst of her dream.

"That's right; come to think of it, in this world, *bodily injury and plunder are impossible...*"

In other words—the things they'd *normally have to watch out for* didn't matter in this world. Perhaps grasping this—no, obviously he grasped it. Quickly *adapting* to this world, Sora smiled ruefully at the peaceful face of his sleeping sister.

"I sure can't beat you in brains…"

—*Knock, knock, knock.* Hearing the gentle sound again, Sora answered.

"Ah, right, yes, who is it?"

"My name is Stephanie Dola. Regarding the matter you spoke to me about during the day…"

…Ste-pha-nie… Oh. He took out his phone and checked the photo he had taken. The classy-looking girl with red hair and blue eyes. That's right, at the tavern downstairs—the one who had been playing a game to be the new monarch or something.

"Ahh. Right, I'm coming."

"…Mng…"

"—Sister, your love makes me delighted to be a brother, but let go of my arm; I can't open the door."

"…?…What…?"

His sister, still looking more than half asleep, finally let go of his arm. Sora peeled his heavy body off the bed, squeaked across the wood floor, and opened the door. The expression he saw on the other side was quite different from the one in the photo on his phone—the Stephanie standing there before him looked crushed.

"—May I enter?"

"Uh, sure, c'mon in."

Going with the flow, he decided to let Stephanie into the room. He offered her the little table and chair in the corner of the cramped room. Sora then sat on the bed with his sister, who was sitting there swaying to and fro, still not quite awake. Stephanie was the one who spoke first.

"…What is the meaning of this?"

"—Of…? Oh, just to make it clear, we're siblings, all right? It's not like—"

"…Geh… Brother rejected mee…"

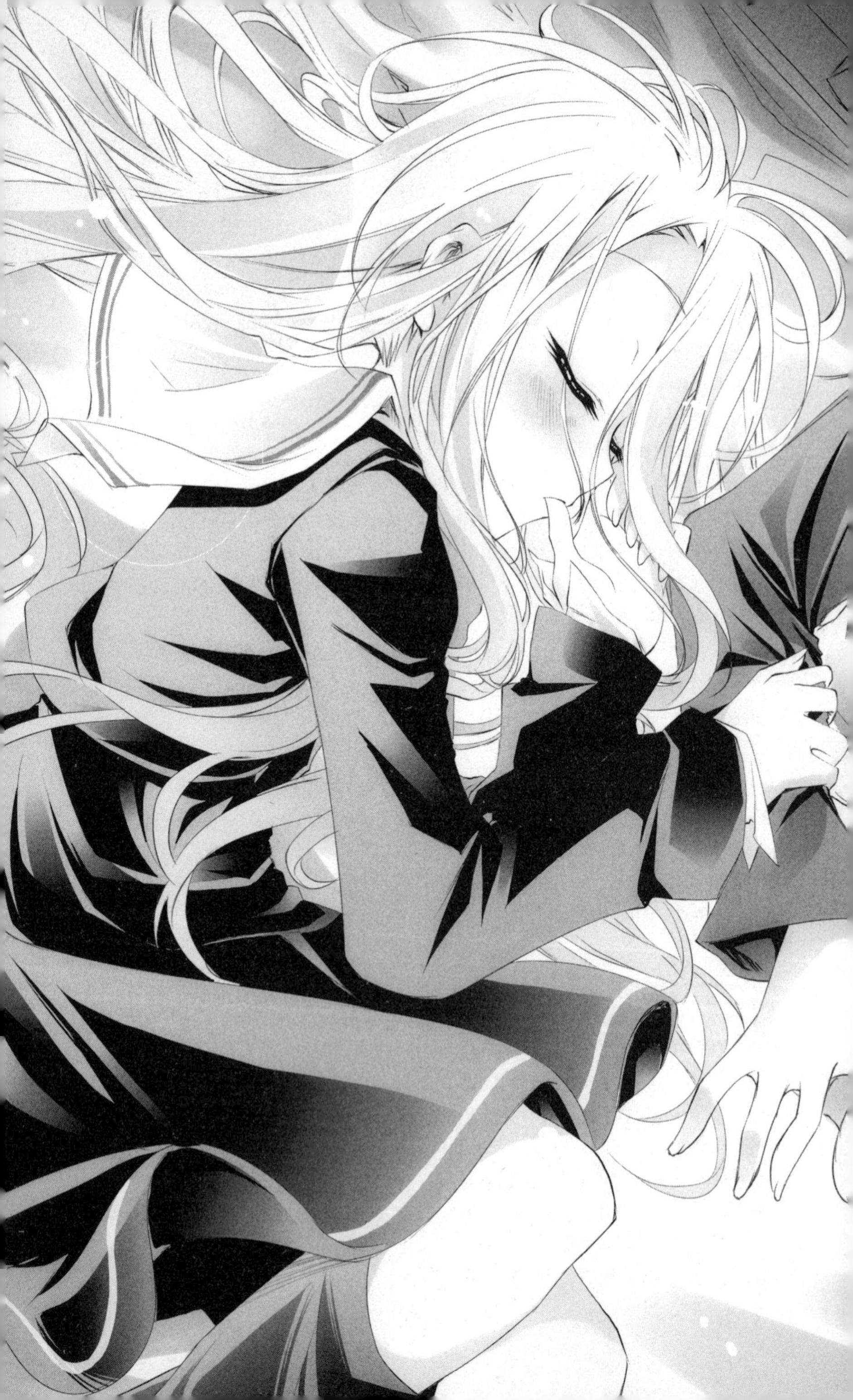

Correction—His sister wasn't half asleep, she was 80 percent asleep, and she was leaning into his back. He didn't know what the manners were like in this world, but he defended himself just in case.

"Uhh, no I didn't. Anyway, I'm Sora. I've never had a girlfriend in my life, and I'm looking!"

"…That is of no concern to me!"

However, seeming to lack the drive to engage the matter, Stephanie continued weakly.

"What concerns me is what happened during the day."

Day—day. What was she talking about? To begin with, what time was it? He didn't see any sunlight from the window, but—. Glancing at his phone, he saw that four hours had gone by since he'd gone to sleep—no wonder he was tired.

"During the day, you told me as you passed by, 'You're being hoodwinked.'"

While making sleepy noises, the sister still perhaps had heard them, for she said with her eyes closed:

"…So…you lost?"

The sister's attitude seemed to strike a nerve.

"Why, yes… Yes, I lost! Now everything is over!"

As Stephanie stood up and cried out, Sora covered his ears.

"Uh, I'm sleep-deprived and you're giving me a headache, so, if you could please not shout so much…"

Stephanie slammed her bag onto the table in a blind rage, apparently having no ears for Sora's modest request. Her shriek rose further.

"If you knew she was cheating, then couldn't you at least have told me how she did it? If I showed everyone, I could have won!"

Remembering the notes he was looking through on his phone before sleeping, Sora said:

"Hmm… The Eighth of the *Ten Covenants*: 'If cheating is discovered in a game, it shall be counted as a loss.' That one."

So just knowing that they were cheating wasn't enough. "Discovered"—it meant *you had to prove they were cheating for it to count as a loss.*

"And now I've lost! Thanks to you, I've been eliminated from the running for the monarch!"

"...In...other words..." Shiro gurgled out a sleepy comment. "...you lost...so you're pissed, and you're taking it out on...us?"

The words showed no intent to cushion their meaning, and Stephanie ground her teeth at their accuracy.

"Oh, Sister. If we're going to throw gas on the fire, let's not pretend to be asleep while we do it."

"...Hmph... What, how'd you know."

"Come on, I know you woke up when I said I'm looking for a girlfriend...We already don't have anyone on our side in this place, you know; we gotta, like, be nice—"

—But. Sora, having said that much, suddenly *got an idea*. Sensing something in the change in her brother's expression, Shiro spoke no more. Meanwhile, as if he'd had a change of personality, Sora's mouth twisted in a grin:

"—Well, my sister is right, after all. It's no wonder the human race is failing."

"...What did you say?"

Stephanie pulled the corners of her mouth taut. But Sora ignored her and intentionally cast his gaze crassly over her body. A frill-covered puff of a dress befitting a princess in a fantasy world was not enough to hide her voluptuous figure as his eyes almost licked over it. *Choosing exactly the words best suited to infuriate her*—he said:

"You couldn't even see through cheating like that, and now you're taking it out on us...and then showing your anger on your face when a little kid calls you out on it—you're such a stooge. If this is the old king's bloodline, no wonder you're failing."

■■■

Sora looked at her with the kind of eyes used to pity an animal of low intelligence. Stephanie's eyes opened wide, and then she glared with an expression trembling in anger.

".........Take it...back."

"Take it back? Ha-ha, what for?"

"Say what you will about me—but I cannot allow you to mock my grandfather!"

Stephanie looked as if about to eat him alive, but Sora just grinned back, even waving his hand.

"You couldn't see her cheating because you were *on the defensive*—people like you who want to win as safely as they can without taking any risks are too busy protecting themselves to actually see what the other player is doing."

Chuckling contemptuously, he let fly.

"Simpleminded, short fuse, no emotional control, conservative. Honestly speaking, you never had a chance."

"—If you'd just shut up and listen to me—!!"

Stephanie got up from her chair looking as if about to grab him, but Sora interrupted.

"Then let's play a game."

"…Uh, um, wha?"

Taken aback. But with unconcealed suspicion, Stephanie listened to Sora's words.

"What, you don't have to think too hard about it. Just rock-paper-scissors. You know it? Rock-paper-scissors."

"Rock—? I, uh…well, certainly."

"Great, *I'm glad to hear you have it in this world, too.* So, we'll play that. But—"

He lifted a finger. Slowly and carefully, Sora explained:

"Not ordinary rock-paper-scissors—you ready? *I'm only going to throw paper.*"

"—What?"

"If I throw anything else, I lose… But, if I throw something else that beats you, you lose, too, so it's a draw—and, of course, if I throw anything else and you have the same thing, then I lose."

"___"

If he throws anything other than paper, he loses? Not comprehending what this man was saying, Stephanie raised her guard still further.

"*—And what is the wager?*"

Sora grinned as if to say—*Glad we could get straight to the point.*

"If you win, I'll do anything and everything you ask. I can explain to you the reason you lost, the truth about the cheating…and if you tell me to die for having insulted *your idiotic gramps*, then that's that."

"……You little…!"

"—And! If I win. *You have to do anything and everything I ask.*"

Sora's face was jovial but colder than ice as it stretched into an unsettling smile. Crudely, repulsively, and—mercilessly, even, he continued:

"I'm putting my life on the line here—surely you don't mind staking your *chastity and such*?"

Stephanie felt the blood that had boiled up to her head draw back with a chill. This did, however, cool her head, and, carefully—she asked:

"—What if…we draw?"

"I'll just give you a hint about the cheating…and, in return…"

Sora made a sudden reversal, smiling while scratching his head bashfully.

"Perhaps you can grant me just one little favor. We should be able to get by for a few days with what we've got—but, to tell you the truth, after our four nights here, we won't have any food or place to stay. We were already worrying about what to do next…"

"—In other words, you want me to provide you with accommodation?"

Sora responded to Stephanie's words with a bubbly smile.

—Was that all? Apparently this guy *just wanted to freeload for a while.*

"What do you saaay? You backing out?"

"……"

"Well, it's true that even if you learn about her cheating now, it's not like you'll get to be queen anymore. I can see you love to play defensively, and there's no real need for you to take such a risk, so you don't have to if you don't want to."

An all-too-blatant provocation. It was too easy to see through—but Stephanie decided to go along with it regardless.

"...Very well, Sir, I shall take you up on your challenge—*Aschente*!"

—This word was an oath signifying a game under the Ten Covenants. An oath to the God that one was ready and willing to follow the Ten Covenants—in a *gamble that was absolutely binding.*

"Okay, then I'm down...*Aschente.*"

Sora made his oath, accompanied by a grin—and a comment that obscured his true purpose. Stephanie, however, was already furiously churning through thoughts in her head.

—He's only going to throw paper? Does he think that if he says that I'm just going to obediently throw scissors? Looking at the conditions he proposed—his intention is obvious. *He's playing for a draw*—that's the only way to look at it. This man *just wants a place to stay*—and *he doesn't even actually know how she cheated.* Surely that was the truth. If he loses if he doesn't throw paper, then the possible outcomes for each of my choices are—Rock: two wins to one loss. Scissors: two wins to one draw. Paper: one win to two draws. After he declared that he'd only throw paper. If I were just going to throw scissors, he'd throw rock. He must be thinking of laughing at me, *Yep, just as I planned; props for innocence, moron.* That said, if I throw paper—I won't lose no matter what. It will almost certainly be a draw, which is just what he wants.

—This cur thinks *there's no way I'll throw rock*—. Because it's the *only way I could lose*!

—Playing me for a fool—! Whether I throw rock or scissors, my odds of winning are two to one. I won't let him have his way—I won't let him have his draw!...Stephanie stared daggers through Sora.

"—!"

—But after glaring at Sora's face, she swallowed. Truly he was a base and contemptible fellow—but that wasn't why. It was his cold, thin smile, *that of a man who calmly knew he was going to win.* Seeing Sora's expression—once again her risen blood dropped as if splashed with cold water.

—No, calm down; think objectively. Stephanie admonished herself and circled her thoughts once more. He'd called her a stooge, emotional, simpleminded—should she allow herself to be provoked by this to prove his point? As she admonished herself thus, Stephanie realized something.

—Of course. It's so obvious. This man—this rogue—has no choice but to throw paper as he declared! *There is no other way he can win.* Which means—no matter what I throw, he can only throw paper as he declared…If he wins, then lucky him, and, *if he draws, it's just as he planned*—that's how it is! *Because he can lose—no matter what he throws!*

"Well, you about ready yet?"

Sora was smiling as if he had already won—but.

"I only await you. Are you prepared to uphold the Covenants?"

Stephanie answered with the same surety of victory. *I can see your hand already—cry out in defeat!*

"Okay, then let's go; yeah, rock, paper—"

—scissors. Was what Stephanie threw. But her eyes.

"Wha——"

———Opened wide at Sora's *rock*.

"Wha-wha—how could…That wasn't…"

"I give you points for not letting yourself be baited and going straight for the rock—but that's not enough."

Wiping his silly grin off his face with ruthless composure Sora calmly adjusted his position on the bed and spoke for Stephanie's inner thoughts.

"You were being baited, *about to throw rock, the only way you could lose.*"

"……—"

"—But then my expression made you calm down and realize that I had no way to win except by throwing paper."

"—Wha—…"

He'd seen through her—wait, so his expression…had been just *acting*?!

"So, that much is fine…but, if you wanted to beat me, you should have thrown paper… Then you would have *destroyed my one chance to win, and had twice as much chance of beating me.*"

—He'd seen through everything—no, *led* everything.

"Ngh—!"

Stephanie bit her lip, folded her knees, and put her hands on the floor. He'd known how she'd calm down—and that on top of that, she'd *go for the win.*

—So this was it. This was the reason Stephanie had lost earlier that day. That seemed to be what he was saying. But he went on.

"Plus, this whole game is stacked for me to win in the first place."

"I know. You wanted to draw. Fine, I'll give you a place—"

Downcast, Stephanie threw this answer back at him—but.

"Yeah, that. That's the thing.—*That's not what I said, you know?*"

"Excuse me?"

"Think back good and carefully. *This* is what I said, yeah?"

—Perhaps you can grant me just one little favor. We should be able to get by for a few days with what we've got—but, to tell you the truth, after our four nights here, we won't have any food or place to say. We were already worrying about what to do next…

"Okay, here's the question! Did I—say *what the little favor was?*"

"……………What?!" protested Stephanie fiercely, bolting to her feet in a panic.

"But—but I asked you, *you want a place, right?!*"

"Yeah, that's the thing…I never said yes."

Stephanie revved her brain full throttle to play back what had happened just moments before. No place to stay, food, what to do next…these words were just decoration. Sora—this guy—had just *smiled.*

—And the one who had *assumed* it meant he wanted to freeload was none other than—

"*Aaaghh.*"

"Now you see! So listen to my little favor request good and carefully!"

With the broadest grin, he pointed at Stephanie with a bang.

"Fall in love with me!"

■■■

………——

……There was a long silence. The one who broke it was the one who had been silently watching the scene play out: Shiro.

"Uhh, Brother?"

"Heh-heh-heh, what is it, my sister? Are you speechless in awe of your brother's perfect plan?"

His sister didn't seem to get it, but Sora went on, drunk on the brilliance of his request. The Sixth of the Ten Covenants—'*Wagers sworn by the Covenants are absolutely binding.*' And, according to the Ninth—they were enforced by the power of the God so as to be impossible to break. Which would mean, of course, that this was *regardless of the individual's will*! But—.

"…Um… What do you mean…?"

Said the sister, still confused. Next it was Sora who looked at her incredulously.

"Oh, my, how unlike you, my little *imouto*."

(He liked to throw in foreign words for effect.)

"It's about the *bonds of love*, you know? If she's bound by the natural laws of this world to uphold the Covenants, we can expect her to fall at my feet, right? Which means we've got our place, we've got money, and even personnel. Three birds with one stone!"

Sora seemed to be asking: You're so smart, why can't you understand that? But Shiro mumbled:

"…Why not…'Be my possession'?"

"——Hm?"

"…Could've got *everything*."

"—Uh, hmm, let's see."

Sora experienced a moment of disorder. And then he sent his thoughts moving at high speed. If, as his sister suggested, he had commanded 'Be my possession,' then *his possession's possessions would all be his automatically*—

"Uh, that's funny? It does sound like that would be…uh."

Why hadn't he thought of it—? She was right. Why was it that when Sora was the one who specialized in this kind of thing, when he was the one who had the ability and the record to back it up, did he—?

"………Brother, your personal feelings?"

"———————Oh…"

Sora looked at at his sister's cold eyes, which were half-shut and probably not just from sleepiness.

"Aaaaaaaaaaaaaaaaaaaaaaaaaaaaaaaaaaaaaaaaaaaaaaaaaaaaaaaaa aaaaaaaaaaaaaaah!"

He grabbed his head and shrieked.

"It—it can't be…could it be?! Can it be that my contemptible fear that if I miss this chance I'll never have a girlfriend for the rest of my life clouded my judgment in the moment when it mattered most?! N-no…It can't—H-how could I make such a—"

Inconceivable. That he himself, the key strategist of "　", could make make such a blunder—it made Sora dizzy. With a sulk in her voice, Shiro continued, even colder.

"…Brother, you said you didn't need a girlfriend… You said…I… was enough."

"I was trying to be cool! I'm sooorrrrrryyyyyyyyyy!"

Sora got down on his hands and knees and bowed his head before his sister, who pouted on the bed.

"Be-because, you know, I can't fool around with my sister! And, anyway, you're eleven years old! The police would come take me away! Your brother's in that time of his life, you know! I'm a young man and I've got…"

The brother filled the air with a barrage of excuses. The sister looked at him unmoved. Meanwhile…

"———"

Stephanie herself—the one of whom the demand had been made—now ignored, looked down and trembled.

Indeed, just as Sora had foreseen, *the Covenants could not be refused.* They were the absolute law of the world. So—her face became hot and her heartbeat wouldn't stop. Her chest was constricted by Sora as he now ignored her and bantered with his sister.

—Even if it was the law of this world. It couldn't be. Not for this guy. Not for this *asshole*.

—She couldn't be—"*jealous*"!

"You really think I'm going along with this?"

"Whoa! Holy shit!"

From her enraged trembling, Stephanie finally burst out and stood up. Glaring keenly at Sora from the stance of resolutely rejecting the feeling that had been planted in her against her will—yet.

"—Ng, nghh!"

As soon as they made eye contact, her heart skipped a beat, and her face got even hotter.

"Wh-wh-whawhawhat part of that is a 'little favor'? Wh-what do you think it means to play with a young girl's heart?!"

While shouting with her eyes averted in a desperate attempt to cover it up. As energetically as she had gotten up, her momentum was flagging.

"Oh, uh… You see, it's…like…"

Sora scratched his cheek, his gaze floating around awkwardly. Though this was just what he'd originally planned, his tremendous oversight had spoiled the mood, and so he contemplated his options.

"Uh, hey, Shiro, what should we do?"

"…Don't ask me…"

"Ngg, ghh…"

He piteously begged his sister for help and was coldly dismissed.

"Ahh!—Ahem!"

Well then—Sora resigned himself to the situation and cleared his throat.

He'd decided to pretend he hadn't made a mistake.

The defiance made Sora feel more comfortable. He smiled frivolously.

"Everyone has their own standards for what's *little*. You have a snack and someone says, can I have a bite of that? and then they *eat the whole thing* and say it was one bite."

Falling back into his groove, Sora returned to spewing such lines.

"That's…that's fraud!"

However, it was of little interest to Stephanie as she argued back.

—Just hearing Sora's voice tickled her. It was a struggle. She'd really have liked him to stop talking, yet she couldn't get enough of hearing his voice. She held it back with the excuse of getting an explanation and continued arguing. Oblivious to Stephanie's girlish dilemma, Sora (eighteen years old, virgin) was calm. He pointed as if to show a student her error.

"Yes, that's just it. You got distracted by the rules of the game and forgot about the *premises*. That's no good, you know, overlooking overly vague statements like that… Even considering that *I intentionally made them hard to see by intimidatingly emphasizing the conditions of victory and defeat*, still, you know?"

—In short, what he was aiming for in this game was a draw. That much Stephanie was right about all along. But that wouldn't get her there. The thing was that, whether it was a draw or a victory—*the risk to Stephanie was the same*. That was the true essence of this game—in other words—

"You, you—swindler!"

That's right. It was a swindle. It was quite reasonable that Stephanie would want to yell this at him—but.

"Whaat, how could you say such a thing? It's your fault for falling for it."

"Th-that's exactly what a swindler would say!"

Hearing Stephanie's argument as it dragged on, Shiro came out from her sulking to finally butt in.

"…Third of the…Ten Covenants… Games…are played for wagers… that each agrees are of equal…value."

Glad to find Shiro finally back on his side, Sora continued.

"That's right! The key word is 'agrees.' Likewise, look at the Fourth: *'Insofar as it does not conflict with Three, any game or wager is permitted.'* Which means?"

Squirming and lifting a finger, Shiro answered.

"…Life, rights—these, too, can be bet…"

"Indubitably, 'tis so! So by the time you're making the wagers, the game's already started."

They made it out to be an explanation to Stephanie, but really it was just more sibling banter. But then, Shiro:

"...But, you didn't have to bet...*feelings*."

"As a matter of fact! This was unavoidable as a way of testing that personal volition does not play a part—"

".........Brother."

"I'm sorry." It seemed that pretending he hadn't made a mistake didn't work on his sister.

"B-but! How dare you—"

How dare he become her first love by such fraud? It was probably cruel to blame Stephanie, who was still trying to argue with tears in her eyes. But:

"...The Sixth of the Ten Covenants... 'Wagers sworn by the Covenants are absolutely binding'..."

The eleven-year-old girl—with pity in her eyes, quietly but accurately hit the mark.

"...Forgetting...the meaning and weight of that, and taking his bait...was your mistake."

—That's right: to begin with, according to the Ten Covenants... Five. *"The party challenged shall have the right to determine the game."* Stephanie had the right to reject the game or change the rules. Those rights had been disregarded to start the game by one person and one person alone—

"——Ngghh..."

—Stephanie herself.

As if she had run out of things to say, Stephanie dropped down and sat on the floor. In fact, the covenant had been made—Stephanie was feeling its effects already. This was proof that *the world recognized the validity of the contest.* No matter what Stephanie said, she had lost, and the wager would be upheld.

"So, uh, I'll take it that you've understood, Stephanie?"

"—*Rgh*... You—!"

You bastard! was what she wanted to scream.

—Her feelings wouldn't let her. What was more, hearing her name called sent a rush of sweet emotion—

"…Nnnmggh, what *iiiiis* this?"

—She bubbled into anger, which caused her to sink down to her knees and elbows and pound her head against the floor.

"Whoa—are—are you okay?!"

"Do I look okay?!"

As Stephanie swung a glare at Sora with her red and swollen forehead, he faltered, but pressed on.

"No, not really. B-but it was me who won the wager, so—I'll proceed to what I want, okay?"

What he wanted——. Right, his goal wasn't *to have her fall in love with him* per se. Now she remembered: It was *to have her fall at his feet.*

But—wait, thought Stephanie. His request was for her to *fall in love with him*. Not to *follow his orders*. That meant Stephanie *had no obligation to accept any further demands from him.*

"Heh…heh-heh-heh, and you thought you'd trapped me…"

That made things simpler. No matter what he asked, all she had to do was shoot back, *No*. That took care of everything!

"Okay, first of all, 'Stephanie' is too long, so can I call you 'Steph' for short?"

"Huh? Uh, sure, I don't mind!——*Hh!*"

—"Steph" nodded happily at having her name shortened. Her decision made seconds earlier that *she wouldn't accept any more demands* was nowhere to be found. There was only a maiden, her cheeks flushing in joy at being given a nickname by her beloved—

"No, it's not—I-I don't care what you c-call me! Yes, that's right, certainly! I still don't have to accept any requests you make after that."

Choosing to force an explanation to herself, Steph still didn't realize *that all she had to do was run out of this room immediately.* Which meant—unconsciously, she'd decided she wanted to be here by Sora's side…

"Right, then you can call me Sora. So, Steph. You're part of the royal family, right?"

—There it was. Indeed, if his goal was for her to fall at his feet: money, housing, food. He'd ask for things like that. However, *there was nothing forcing Steph to answer these demands.* Steph snickered inwardly. Sora would come asking, and she'd just say straight out, "I refuse!" That swindler would realize his blunder—what a sight his face would be. Holding that line ready, Steph waited for Sora's demand.

"Then you must have a big house. Can we live there together for a while?"

"——Oh, yes, of course. ♥"

——…

What?

"Uh, what? I, what?"

Steph entered a state of confusion at her own remarks. But she considered her face, which was heating up enough to give her a nosebleed. Sora's words:

"Can we live there together?"—

In short, he meant, well, living together. He meant sharing a roof…*cohabitating.* Which meant always being together. Which meant…sharing a bed, a bath—

"Ah, ah, aaaaaaaaah, no, no, it's not like that!"

As Steph bashed her head against the wooden wall, Sora inquired sheepishly, his face pale. "Uh, um, you're, like, wow, I don't… It's not okay, then?"

"Of *course* it's *okay*!—Aahhh… There's no use…" Steph looked at the ceiling with a humorless smile.

—Indeed, Sora had made a spectacular mistake. A request with no contractual force. But Sora (who had never had a girlfriend in his life) and Steph (who had just been forced to experience her first love)…

…had treated the fact that history had seen nations fall over a single love much too lightly.

■■■

"Heh, heh-heh… I…don't care anymore; you can do whatever you want with me…"

Steph groveled, weeping, on the floor. Sora's request may not have had any contractual force, but it was too late for her to do anything about it. Finally realizing this, Steph could only say this with empty eyes, with half a smile.

"—Do you have any other requests? Heh-heh, just tell me your damned wish."

But having come this far, it must be said that Steph's forethought was insufficient. She had not contemplated *the most logical request* to follow "Fall in love with me."

"Uh, well, I guess…"

Sora glanced at Shiro. Steph had no way of knowing what that glance meant. But Shiro nodded.

"…It's okay… I would feel sorry for you…if you had to wait, until I was…eighteen."

"Can you not talk about feeling sorry for me? Also, you know your brother's not going to mess around with his sister."

"…That's why."

Shiro stuck her thumb between her index and middle fingers without expression.

"…Brother, grats on losing your virginity."

"——Wha—"

—Yes. Perhaps she'd been raised too well, or perhaps her imagination just wasn't powerful enough, but the obvious idea that he would *seek her body* once more lit the eyes of Steph, who had surrendered entirely.

"Wha-whawha-what? Y-y-you never said anything about…! Y-y-you've got to set up the mood for these things, do it in the right place at—uh? Huh?"

But where the light returned was not the fear of her chastity being threatened—but the *anticipation* of it—and as soon as Steph realized as much, she went back to trying to dig a hole in the wall with her head. Sora, showing no signs of recognizing the subtleties of Steph's heart in these distressing matters, spoke plainly.

"No. We can't have any R-18 scenes until you're eighteen, Shiro."

"—Eh?"

Steph mumbled. But, of course, no one paid attention to her.

"...I don't mind."

"Well, your brother does! Pornography is bad for kids. It's absolutely unacceptable!"

"...I thought you just told her to fall in love...because you don't like the sick and twisted genre..."

"Um, excuse me, why is it you know all about your brother's sexual proclivities?"

"...You've got...all your game boxes in the room...they're everywhere..."

Steph had no idea what they were talking about, but she could certainly recognize when she was being ignored.

—And that, for some reason, they were assuming that the sister would have to be there.

"—Um, couldn't you just have your sister leave the room?"

"Hm? I'm glad to hear you're looking forward to it, but there are certain reasons that's not going to work."

"—That's not—! That's not what I meant, stupid! Don't be crazy!"

Disregarding the red-faced Steph, like scholars who had hit upon a major problem and were searching for a solution, the pair folded their arms and pondered, which finally sparked an apparent realization.

"...In that case," Shiro explicated the merciless solution. "...You can...*push the envelope.*"

"Ohh, that's it! That's my sister, the genius girl!"

".......Huh?"

Sora was doting on his sister, and the sister seemed to be enjoying it. And—somehow. They seemed to have "*found a way for things to go there*" with the sister present. Steph tensed.

"—But how far can we go, I wonder?"

"...Brother, you're the expert on that..."

"*That*—if that's a reference to manga and games, I should point out that things don't work the same way in real life, my dearest little sister."

"You don't...know what to do...because you're a virgin?"

As Sora showed his appreciation for her appropriate but unnecessary translation, Shiro waved her smartphone.

"I'll record it with my camera…and tell you what to do."

"Hm. Setting the idea of telling me what to do aside for a moment, why do you need to record it, my little sister?"

"…Brother, you don't want…pr0n?"

"Hmm. I am puzzled by my sister's unusual consideration but shall gratefully accept it."

With complex feelings, Sora turned back to Steph. Steph, meanwhile, just stared, not knowing what the smartphone was. Shiro started recording video and gave her first direction.

"Take one. He trips, and he falls down…like…?"

"Oh—*that* scene. But…how am I supposed to fall down in this—"

As Sora looked around for something to "trip" on, Shiro crept up—"…Hmp."—And kicked him lightly.

"Whoa—I get it! (*Monotone*) Ooops, I'm faalliing."

"———Eh?"

With acting that wouldn't even qualify as third-rate, Sora fell unnaturally onto Steph. When they landed, his hands were placed—

—of course, right on her breasts. He could have ordered Steph to interpret the situation as a mere "cliché"—but that would have been abusive, obviously.

"…Take two…Breast fondling due to an act of God…"

"Uh…How is it an act of God if I'm…"

"…Okay, never mind…"

"No, let's do it, Director. I'll do my best!——*Hi-yah!*"

Squish, squish. Squoosh, squoosh. Squish, squish. Squoosh, squoosh. Foomp, foomp. Boink, boink, boink, boink. Foomp, foomp. Boink, boink, boink, boink. Jiggle, jiggle. Bounce, bounce. Bwwwwooooing.

"Whoa…"

Sora could only think of an interjection to describe the feeling that was just as rich as he expected. Meanwhile, Steph was dumbfounded, with her eyes open wide. Her comprehension could not keep up with the situation—at least, that was certainly a factor.

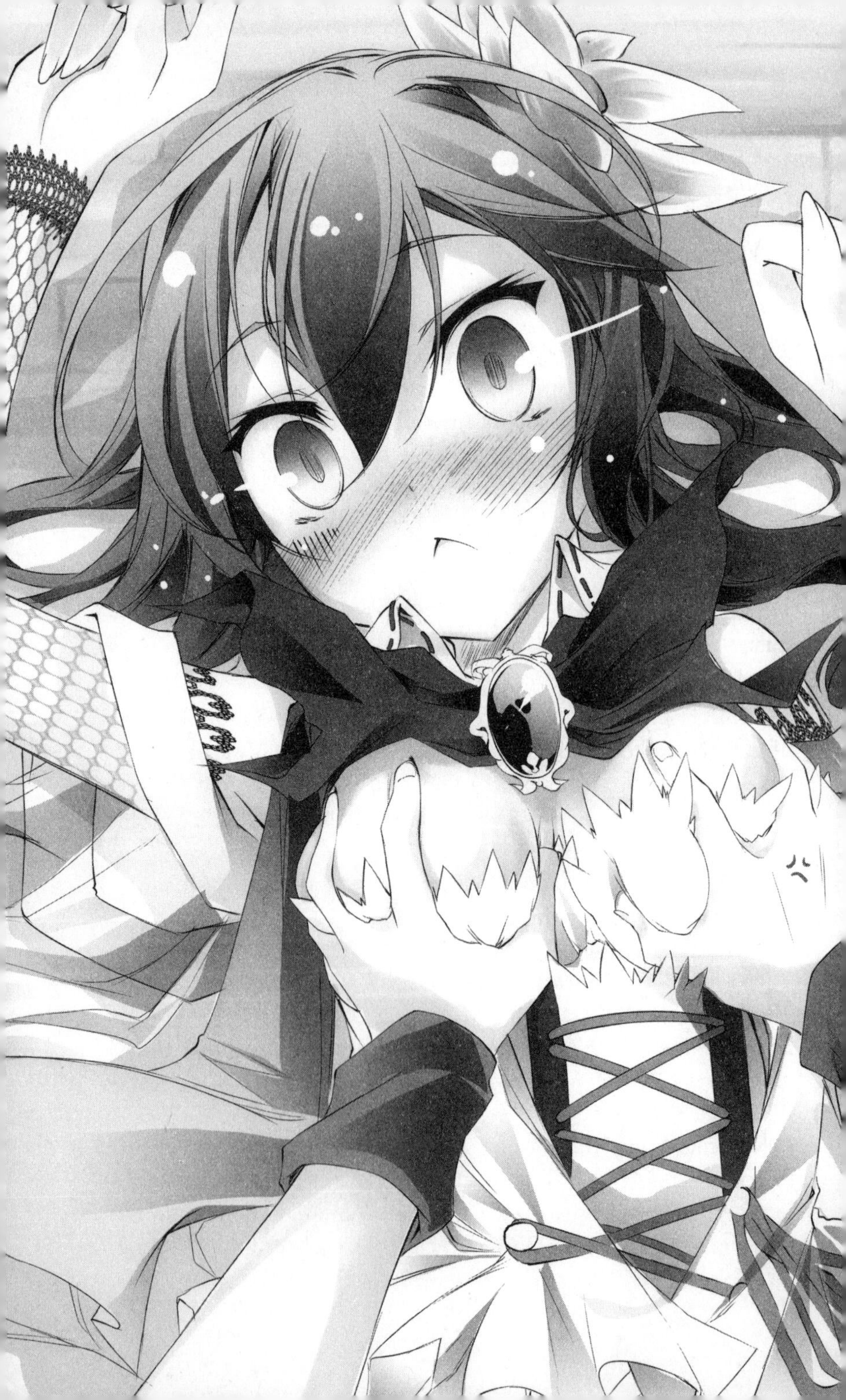

More importantly, the sensation of his hands on her *gave her a feeling that somehow melted her thoughts.*

"—O...h!"

A moan escaped Steph's lips, but, fortunately, perhaps because she covered it, the two didn't hear it.

"—Hm-hmmgh... Th-three-D girls are actually not bad...Uh—excuse me, Director. Is this still going to be rated All Ages?"

"Sure...but, Brother...you're overdoing it."

Shiro knit her brows slightly, looking down at her own flat chest.

"Oh—that's true. The breast fondling is purely an accident, so it would be better to limit it to three panels or so—so, uh, what shall we do next, Director?"

"...Take three. The ensuing breast slip."

"Wait, is that okay?"

Sora objected without thinking, but Director Shiro answered seriously and decisively.

"...By *J*mp* standards, even full frontal nudity...is nothing."

"Wait, no, she can't be naked! In real life, there are nipples, you know?"

"...Well, that's...added in the trade paperbacks..."

"Director, this is real life. This is happening in real life. We can't white them out or redraw them."

"...Then...underwear?"

"Well, sure—but I'm not sure how her clothes could come off in this situation."

Sora and Shiro felt the pain of the disparity between the real world and fiction.

"...Brother, what if...we were talking, about the bottom."

"Oh, I see, a flash from a skirt flip! You're right, Director, that's totally okay for all ages!"

Then, as Sora reached to flip Steph's skirt, a spark lit up Steph's melted brain.

—Skirt...flip? Underwear—Are they talking about *seeing my panties*?

—No, that's not okay. My top is okay. Well, not really, but. Steph was warned not by her barely remaining reason, but by her instincts: The bottom is *not okay*. Not okay. Definitely not okay. At the very least, *not okay right now*. It was— Well, how best to put it?

—It might have been a planted emotion. But, being pushed down and breast-fondled by the one she loved, there were certain *physiological changes* that inevitably happened.

"—Eep—Aaaaaaah?!"

This instinct thrust Steph's frazzled brain into action. Quickly, she swept away the arm Sora was touching her with and pushed him away.

"Whoa!"

Since Sora had crouched to flip her skirt, one push from a woman was enough to throw him off balance. He stood up in a struggle not to fall over, but it only made things worse. The distance he was falling lengthened, and he was forced to take a few steps back.

—Which brought him to the door. The single light push from Steph carried him until—. *Gonk*. A dull noise.

"Oww!"

Sora raised his voice upon hitting his head.

—But that wasn't the end of it.

—Ah, low-cost lodging. The impact flicked open the cheap door fitting, and Sora fell straight into the hall.

"…Brother!"

"—Huh—hey, what—!"

And, so as to close off the voices of the two concerned about Sora. *Creeeee*…went the cheap metal—*Wham*. From the recoil of its opening the door swung quietly closed.

——……

For a moment, Steph was stunned, not understanding what had just happened. But then, realizing that her one push had thrust Sora out into to the hall of the inn.

"—*Hh!* So-Sora?!"

She called his name for the first time as she hurried to her feet.

There was a sensation of tightness in her chest, and a powerful feeling of unease. She decided to assume it was just concern that she might have hurt someone with her actions. As for the possibility that it was worry that he might not like her anymore—that, she flatly refused to accept. While thus reassuring herself, she rushed to open the door and flew out into the hall.

There, in the corner of the hall, Sora was clutching his head and shaking.

"Wha——!"

She didn't think she had pushed him hard enough that he'd fall all the way over there. But there he was, in the corner of the hall.

"So-Sora?! A-are you okay?"

He was clutching his head. He had hit his head hard against the door, but it couldn't be—Steph paled. But—

"I'm sorry I'm sorry I'm sorry forgive me forgive me please forgive me—"

—It seemed it wasn't because he'd hit his head. Still, Sora was just crouching and apologizing over and over.

"——Pardon?"

"I'm sorry I'm sorry I mean I thought if I missed this chance I'd never have a chance to touch a boob my whole life I mean I'm a guy and I do want a girlfriend and I do have dirty thoughts and no really I get it so please don't look at me with those disdainful eyes yes I'm awful yes I'm a pervert yes I know I'm sorry I'm so sorry—"

—After cheating her and sexually harassing her, standing unashamed throughout, now Sora shook like a newborn lamb as he apologized.

"…Wh-what's this about?"

Steph had no idea what was going on. She peeked back into the room, thinking she could ask his sister, Shiro, for an explanation.

"………Brother…Brooother… Where arrre you… Don't, leave me, a…looone…"

—Shiro, on the bed, was just like her brother: crouching with her knees in her arms, trembling visibly, dropping tears without expression.

"——Wh-what's going on with these two?"

By now, Steph had forgotten all about having had her breasts grabbed, and all she could do was stare.

——…

Yes, this was " ": Sora and Shiro. The *"two-in-one"* player. It wasn't just about having different skills. If they were separated too far—in other words. It was because *one was so socially phobic she couldn't even communicate*——and the other was so *socially maladjusted* that he was beyond hope.

"…Brother…Brother, where arrre you…"

"I'm sorry I'm sorry I'm sorry I'm sorry…"

Are things making sense now? A loser. A shut-in. The two siblings, separated by seven years, could only be in the same place *at home*—. This—explained everything.

⏻ CHAPTER 2 CHALLENGER

In the Kingdom of Elkia, the capital, Elkia—specifically, Block 3 of the Western District. The siblings had checked out of the inn, where they had more or less blackmailed the innkeeper into letting them stay several nights, without staying a single one. Now they greeted a new morn at Stephanie Dola's house. Or to be more precise—at the bath.

"…Brother, please, explain."

Shiro was naked, and her head was being washed.

"Explain? If we're pushing the envelope, we've gotta have a bath scene. What more explanation you need?"

"…Brother… Bath scenes are…censored… Elementary schoolkids… are totally off-limits."

"Worry not, my sister, Mr. Steam is on the job, so we'll just be pushing the envelope."

Thus declared Sora as he viewed the grand bath, unnaturally full of rising steam.

"Could it be that this is the only reason you ordered me to boil the grand baths?"

Steph washed Shiro's hair, aghast.

"What do you mean, the only reason? It's important."

"Do you know how much firewood the staff wasted for that?"

In addition, of course, it was impossible to get into a bath that was boiling. They had also wasted water to raise the steam…

"If you want to go there, what about you, using this huge bath all by yourself?"

"—Nggh…"

This was perhaps what it meant to be part of the royal bloodline. Steph was even richer than Sora had imagined. Her mansion, built in a style vaguely reminiscent of Rome, was so big that the siblings, who had known only Japan, would have believed it if told it was a castle. Steph's private bath, which they were using now, seemed spacious enough for ten people to use. The bath, also reminiscent of Rome in its furnishings, was steamed up to be appropriate for all ages and was so magnificent that it was impossible to think that humans were in decline after losing so many games.

"Ah, excuse me. My sister hates baths—and she always fusses, 'You can't show naked eleven-year-olds even if it's R-18!' and won't let me wash her, so she doesn't get bathed much. After she suggested pushing the envelope yesterday, I thought I'd better take advantage of it."

"…Nggh… Brother, I hate you."

It was about pushing the envelope on Steph. That was Shiro's subtext.

"My sister, if you do things right, you'll be a dazzling beauty, so do things right."

"…I don't have to be…a beauty."

"Your brother likes the beautiful Shiro betterrr."

"…Ngghhh…"

Shiro groaned as if that meant something, but didn't end the discord.

—That didn't really matter. Well, it was a little annoying how close they were, but setting that aside, there was a more important question that couldn't be ignored.

This situation. The event that was currently transpiring. Why was she washing a naked Shiro's hair, *while a clothed Sora was behind her with his back turned*?

"—Sora…why do I have to be *naked and washing Shiro's hair*?"

—No, don't all chime in. *Why, then, had she not refused?* She was well aware of her responsibility in this matter.

"Weren't you listening to me? Because this is the only way Shiro will take a bath."

"Wha—so, you don't care about me?!"

"Hm? You want me to look?"

"Of—of course not! I'm asking you if this is harassment!"

"Don't worry, Steph. I intend to view your naked body carefully by *other means*."

"—Wha—"

As soon as she heard this, she flushed red and hid her body. At the same time, at hearing Sora suggesting that he did have some interest in her, she felt *relief*. Steph looked around for a wall to bash her head against, but then Sora spoke up apologetically.

"However, for now you must forgive me—I cannot rely too fully on Mr. Steam."

"......Excuse me?"

"For instance, if I should join you in the bath only for my indolent member to suddenly regain motivation, or if Mr. Steam should fail to perform as hoped in preventing me from viewing my young sister directly, it won't be R-18; it will be banned."

"—Uh, I see."

She didn't, really, but Sora seemed to be saying that he didn't need to look right now.

The limits of Steph's comprehension here were perhaps unavoidable. Set up in the bath were two phones and a tablet. Steph had no way of knowing the meaning of those little cameras.

—Later Sora would have Director Shiro check the footage and show it to him if it seemed acceptable. Sora swore this in his heart and repressed his urge to turn around.

■■■

"*Hff*... That hits the spot..."

"Mngh... My hair's all papery... It's itchy..."

Sora had waited for Shiro to get out of the bath and then taken a quick shower. Sora was refreshed, having finally gotten a chance to wash himself. Shiro spoke to him crossly.

—Sora had been right, after all, about how Shiro looked when her hair was washed and nicely combed. Her tresses made a gentle wave, looking soft to the touch and white as snow, and further brought out her porcelain-white skin—along with her round face, balanced features, and red eyes, she was like a doll made by a master of the craft.

"If only you could be like that all the time; it's such a waste."

"…It's not like anyone but you…is gonna see."

Sora, too, had just finally shaved and despite his teasing was also looking sharper. How to put it? *I—I blew it*, thought Steph when she looked directly at him; she could hardly stop herself from getting a nosebleed, it was so… His initial scruffiness had been alleviated, and now he had the clean freshness of a "fine young man."

But—that wasn't the problem. Steph desperately struggled to stop blood from dripping from her nose.

"Y-y-you two—put on some clothes!" she shouted at the towel-clad, *half-naked siblings* as they looked on blankly.

"…You're the one who told us to send them for cleaning. Those are all we've got; are they dry already?" Sora asked, doubting that this world had dryers.

To which Steph replied, "Th-th-th-that's… Fine, then, I'll get you something else—I-I wonder if I have any gentlemen's clothes… Ng, nghh… Why do I have to be…"

Steph turned, muttering to herself, to look for clothes.

——And ten minutes later. In the same location as before, Steph had fallen to her knees and hung her head, experiencing massive regret.

I—I blew it……!

"O-ho, so this is a butler's outfit—what you call a tailcoat… It's a bit formal, but it's like cosplay, so it's fun! Shiro, you look good in that, too."

"…Too many frills. Hard to move…"

Shiro was clad in a dress that Steph had worn as a child.

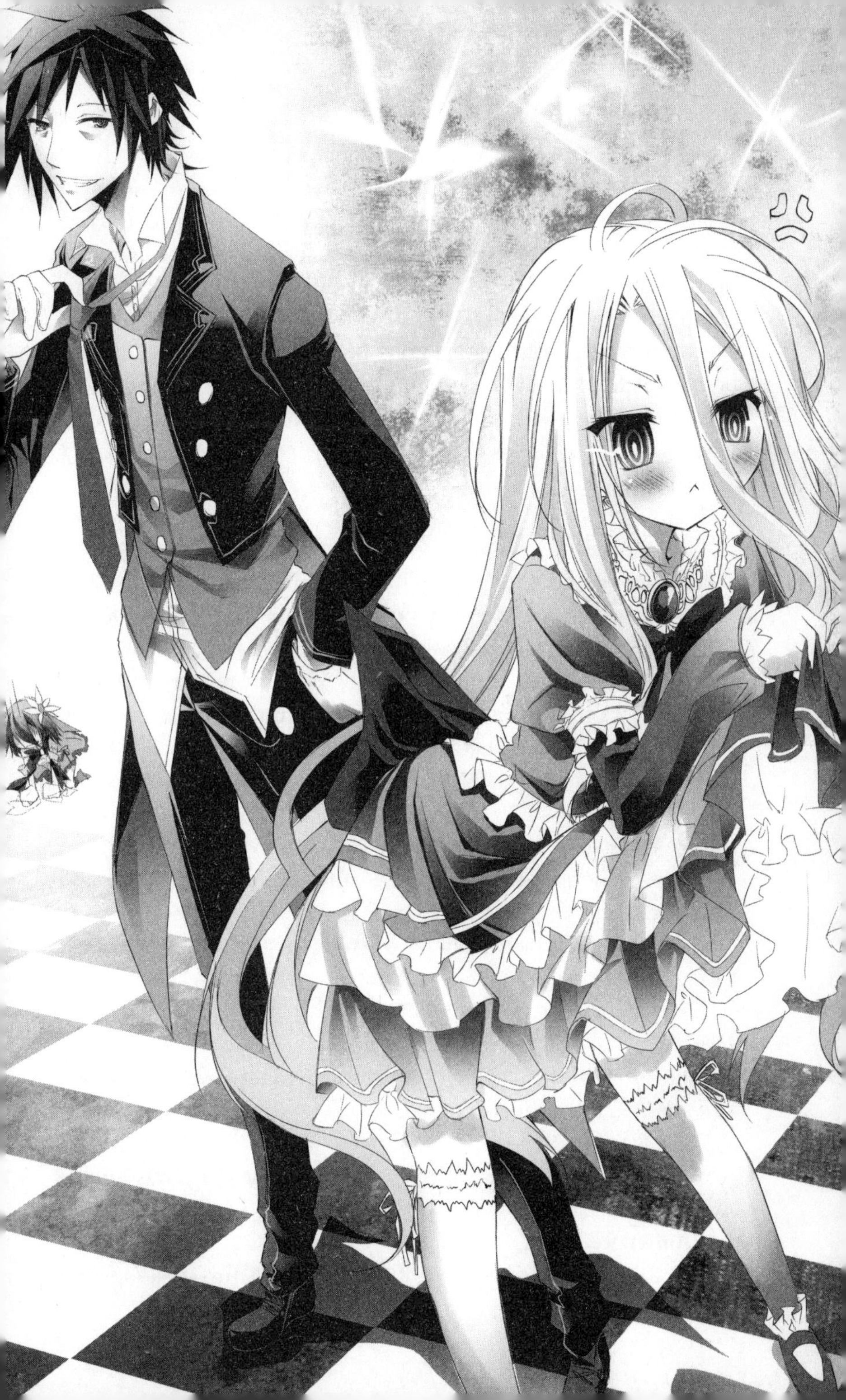

It was all very well that Steph had gone out to look for clothes to fit the half-naked pair. But she had no men's clothes, so she had to use the staff's—in other words, a butler's outfit. Likewise, the only clothes she could find to fit an eleven-year-old girl were hers from her childhood. Now the siblings looked like a well-bred young lady and her faithful butler—

Glance. Steph looked once more. Sora's wide shoulders and thin body somehow fit all too well as a butler, which sent Steph's heart racing. And with the way his sister looked in charge of him, Steph's heart twinged for the third time.

"I blew it…"

"Huh? Blew what?"

"Never mind!"

Panicking at the sincerity that had slipped out of her mouth, Steph shook her head as she swept up her knees from the floor and got up.

If Sora had been attuned to such maidenly subtleties, he wouldn't have been a virgin for eighteen years. "Well, then," he murmured. "Now that we've got our sleep and freshened up in the bath—Steph."

"Uh, um, yes? Wha-what is it?"

"What are you so flustered about? Does this house…mansion—castle…?"

Born and raised in Tokyo, Japan, Sora couldn't seem to find a category to fit Steph's dwelling, so he came to the conclusion that it didn't matter.

"Does this place have a library or study or something, someplace we can do research?"

"Uh, yes…it does…but why?"

"Are you hard of hearing, Stephy-poo? Of course, for *research*?"

"I-I heard that! I'm asking what you want to research!"

"What… This world, of course."

"'This world'…?"

Steph stood bewildered at his suggestion that there was *another world*.

"Brother, we haven't…told her."

As if still dissatisfied with her dried-out hair, Shiro spoke sullenly.

"—Hm? What? Is that so?"

"Sorry, but…I'm not seeing what this is about."

"Ah, right. It's tricky to find the words to explain when the subject gets brought up so formally."

It was that classic event in *this kind of story* where the protagonist was bottlenecked by others' inability to believe them. Sora carefully searched for the right words to make her believe.

—Scratching his head, sighing. Making a clearly bothered face. Awkwardly, casually, he let it out.

"Basically, we're *people from another world*. So we want to know more about this world."

The study—no. A *library* about the size of a high school's. Steph had led them to her *personal study*, filled with neatly lined bookshelves, reams of books covering the walls. It did seem perfect for research, but—

"Hey, Steph."

"Yes? What is it?"

Sora had hit upon one large, unexpected obstacle.

"*—Is this country's official language not Japanese?*"

Sora groaned with an illegible book in his hand, holding his head.

"Ja-pa-nese? I'm not sure what you're talking about, but, naturally Immanity uses the Immanity tongue."

"Whoa… This world is so simple."

The problem was that even though somehow Sora and Shiro were able to converse with the people of this world, the characters written in the book made no sense at all.

"So, you really did come from another world."

"Yeah, well, I'm not really expecting you to believe us—"

Sora knew they wouldn't be believed right away, so he wasn't even bothering to try.

"Oh, no, it's not all that surprising."

Steph's nonchalant answer took Sora aback. "What? Why not?"

Now Steph went blank. "Why not? I don't know. Some of the advanced magic used by the Elves includes otherworldly summons. It's not implausible that you might be like that. To begin with, I can see from your clothes and faces that you're not from this country, but you're you're still Immanities no matter how you look at it…"

—And this was, after all, the only human country left.

"Ah…I see. This is a fantasy world… *Hh.*"

Having had his expectations upturned, Sora sighed. He turned back to the illegible book and scratched his head.

"Hmm, but it's still quite inconvenient not to be able to gather information by ourselves. Can you learn it…Shiro?"

"…Mm."

"Yeah?"

"…Mm."

It seemed that the siblings were conducting some kind of communication that made sense only to them. They quietly cast their eyes on the book and fell silent. With this stillness in the corner of her eye, Steph sighed.

"…And what do you want me to do?"

She added sarcastically that she could fall at his feet as a home tutor, but Sora made a different request, his eyes never leaving the book.

"No. There's something else."

Sora's words reminded Steph of last night, and this morning, and she braced herself, preparing not to be surprised at whatever perverted request was coming—

"Can you just answer me a few questions for now?"

"—Um…uh, sure. That's…quite all right."

Steph felt the load come off her chest with this unexpectedly decent request. Sora asked with a perfectly serious face.

"You know, yesterday, why was it that when I fondled your breasts, you didn't resist, but when I tried to flip your skirt, you suddenly— all right, never mind, I'll ask a serious question. I was just joking…"

On the receiving end of Steph's piercing glare, Sora looked back down at the book.

"Hmm, okay, so, I keep hearing this word 'Immanity,' but what does it contrast to?"

Steph queried back as if this was a totally unexpected question. "…Weren't there any other races in your world?"

"Well, humans were the only ones we could communicate with, at least—so."

"Uh, well… Yes…"

Considering where she should begin if they really were from another world as they said, Steph began.

"First—are you familiar with *myth*?"

"You mean how the Ten Covenants came to be? I heard it from a minstrel who was playing by a fountain."

"Very well—in that case—"

—*Ahem.*

"'Races' refers to the intelligent *Ixseeds*, to whom the God's Ten Covenants apply."

"'Exceeds'…"

"War ended in this world when the Ten Covenants came to prohibit all violation of rights, bodily injury, violence, and slaughter among the Ixseeds."

"…I see. I was wondering what you guys ate—but the Covenants only apply to intelligent life, huh?"

Sora appeared to be reading the book but was still grasping her words clearly. While inwardly marveling at his dexterity, Steph continued.

"However—perhaps I should call it *war by games*. Basically, struggle for territory—'play for dominion' still continues."

"Play for dominion"—Sora recognized the term.

"—Is this the only Immanity nation?"

"…As of now, yes… It's not as if it's a requirement that each race have only one nation—but Elkia is the last bastion of Immanity."

—Having heard that much, Sora went ahead and presented a question to which he already knew the answer. To compare basic assumptions between *this world and their own*, in other words.

"Why do you still fight over domain when there are no more wars? Can't you settle it by talking?"

"Uh, well, that's…"

But, in place of the faltering Steph, the sister answered.

"…Resources are finite… Living things can multiply infinitely… Dividing a finite quantity by an infinite quantity…destroys everything."

"…Y-yes. Exactly!"

Steph jumped on the pronouncement of the sister, who had answered before her, and nodded hurriedly.

"…Come on, I know you didn't think of that…"

Sora looked as Steph as if disgusted by her input, rendered useless by his sister's prompter response.

"Whawhawha-what are you saying; it's so basic!"

—Well, this was a world where that was how things were since birth. The question of why living things would play games to *take from each other*, while perhaps considered, might be difficult to answer.

"Anyway, this is pretty much like our world in that respect, after all."

Sora sighed. Though *combat* had vanished, *conflict* remained.

—So, perfect equality was impossible. Musical chairs, after all, was a game about fighting for limited seats. In this way, the majority would draw the lot of poverty for the minority to prosper—really, nothing had changed between this world and their own……

"…So, what kinds of races do the *Ixseeds* include?"

Sora cut his thinking short and returned to the conversation. Steph counted with her fingers uncertainly as she recalled what she'd had to memorize.

"Rank One is Old Deus, defeated by the One True God; Rank Two is Phantasma; Rank Three is Elemental—and there's Dragonia and Gigant…and Elf and Werebeast—and so forth."

"…I see, so pretty much your typical fantasy world."

Sora mumbled his feedback to Steph's "and so forth," amused that she'd given up on remembering all sixteen races, when something suddenly occurred to him.

"Hey, what do you mean…'Rank'?"

"Uh, well. I don't know that much about it, either, but apparently there's a *ranking*."

"—Ranking?"

"Yes, basically it's based on their magical aptitude scores, I hear."

"'Apparently, basically, I hear'… You don't really know what you're talking about, do you? Steph, did you study up on this stuff properly?"

As Sora put his loser self on a pedestal, Steph grimaced, muttered an irritated "Fine already," and cleared her throat.

"I'll have you know, I graduated from the academy just fine! Human research still just hasn't made much progress on the ranking—because Immanity is Rank Sixteen. That is, we have *a magical aptitude score of zero*. As much as we'd like to research it, *we have no way of observing it*."

"…Zero?" Sora asked, looking up from his book.

"Hm—? Wait a sec, *humans can't use magic*?"

"That's right. We can't even detect magic."

"…What about if you, like…use an item or something?"

"We can use games created with magic…but it's just the game working by its magic—humans can't use magic themselves."

"—And this principle is absolute?"

Sora interrogated her persistently, but Steph didn't seem to get offended. Rather—

"It is. *Spirit corridors*—Immanity lacks these circuits to connect to the source of magic." Steph lowered her face a bit. "That's why we lose in the play for dominion, you see…"

—Hmmm. Sora gave a dry smile and pressed on.

"…So, in that case, who's the best at magic? Rank One, right?"

"Oh, no, actually. If you go that high, they're gods—their very being is a kind of magic. If you speak of being good at magic in the common sense, the best would be Rank Seven, Elf."

Elf. The stereotypical image rose in his mind.

"—Elf… By Elf, you mean the pale guys with the pointy ears?"

You're certainly knowledgeable for someone from another world, said Steph's expression. "Yes, indeed. Currently, Elven Gard is the largest nation in the world. They've used their magic to climb their way to the top. If you say 'magic,' you think of Elves."

—"Hm," puffed Sora. Placing his hand on his chin and thinking, looking into space with a gaze that could not be more serious.

"—!"

Her heart pounded at his serious profile and his tailcoat-clad aura of composure. *It's an illusion it's an illusion it's an illusion—it's a planted emotion!* Steph chanted to herself as if casting a spell. Meanwhile, Sora seemed to have got his thoughts together. Choosing his words as if probing for something, he queried.

"…Are there any races that can't use magic…but still have large nations?"

"Uh, well, now that you mention it, Rank Fourteen, Werebeast, can't use magic…"

Stammering, Steph somehow managed to answer.

"On the other hand, it's said they have extraordinary senses, with which they can sense the presence of magic and read people's minds. The Werebeasts have united their islands in the Great Ocean to the southeast into the Eastern Union, which has already become the third-largest nation in the world—"

Steph continued painfully, unconsciously squeezing her arm with the hand she had on it.

"…Indeed, that is a race and nation which, unable to use magic itself, has—not overcome, but at least come to rival Elven Gard with powers beyond the reach of Immanity. But the other side of it is that it was all accomplished using powers that, from the point of view of Immanity, are still supernatural or extrasensory."

"—Hmm. That's interesting."

Humans couldn't use magic, nor could they even tell if it had been used. There could be no victory when the other side was cheating in a way that was impossible to catch.

—*If that was what they thought, then, yeah, they would lose.*

"I see…I see how it is."

Just about as Sora was nodding deeply, as if everything made sense.

"…Brother—I've learned it."

Shiro's voice rang out.

"Oh, that's my sister."

"…Praise me, more…"

"Of course, of course. That's my sister; I'm so proud of you, you genius girl you! Wuzzawuzzawuzza."

Sora stood and messed up Shiro's hair as she squinted with pleasure like a cat.

—Steph looked on, uncomprehending.

"…Huh? Learned what?"

"Learned what? *The Immanity tongue*, of course."

Sora looked blankly at Steph and tossed his words off casually.

"But, yeah, you're so awesome. It's still gonna take me a little while longer."

"…Brother, you're slow."

"Heh-heh-heh, it's better for a man to be slow than fast, you know?"

"…Brother, you're so small."

"Nn-n-n-n-n-no, I'm not!! H-how do you even——Steph, what's up?"

Steph was watching their banter agape. She spoke in a falsetto.

"Excuse me…did I hear you correctly? Did you say—*she learned a whole language*?"

"Um? Yeah, so?"

Shiro nodded once in agreement.

"—In—this short time? You're kidding, right?"

Steph checked again with a strained face. Sora answered carelessly.

"It's not that big a deal. As far as we've spoken, our grammar and vocabulary is exactly the same. All we need to learn is your writing system and we're done."

"…And…you still haven't learned it, Brother."

"I can't learn it in fifteen minutes. That's crazy. I'm not as smart as you; give me another hour. Anyway, what is this? I can't figure out the pattern for how this symbol is used—"

"Don't, think of that, like Japanese… Think of it like a Romance language…"

"No, I mean, I thought of that, but, then, look at the grammar; the predicate would be in the wrong position…"

"…Classical Chinese…"

"What? It's inverted only in writing? What a pain in the ass—oh, but, yeah, that does work."

"…Brother, learn more languages…"

"Come on, you're the special one who can speak *eighteen languages* including their classical forms. Your brother's a mundane who only knows *six languages*, but that's enough for gaming."

Steph watched this banter incredulously. But the siblings didn't seem to think anything of it, and tossed it around like it was all in a day's work. But it was true that the words and speech were the same; all they had to do was learn the writing system. Ah, you might say, when you lay it out, it shouldn't be that hard after all. But you have you noticed that they were working with another important factor? That is—.

To do that without being taught by anyone wasn't *learning*, it was *deciphering*.

And accomplishing that in such a short time wasn't even something to brag about for them. (Was this normal in their world?) Two beings that had already completely overturned her understanding. Looking at the otherworldly siblings, Steph felt a chill run down her spine—but also a heat that built faintly in her heart.

…Could it be? Perhaps she really had met people who were completely beyond this world.

People—*who could change this nation.*

"—Hm? What is it?"

Steph's heart jumped at Sora, who turned as if he'd noticed her eyes.

"Ah, um, no, it's—I'm gonna make some tea."

As Steph scuttled out of the library, her ears looked slightly reddish. Watching uncertainly, Sora wondered.

"…What's up with her?"

While Shiro went on reading without so much as a glance.

"…Brother, you don't…understand…girls."

"—Yes, that's why I've been a virgin for eighteen years. Wait, does that even have anything to do with it?"

Here was an eighteen-year-old man being lectured about feminine psychology by his eleven-year-old sister. They do say that boys mature emotionally slower than girls... In this case, at least, that seemed to be a fact.

"...Even though...you're better than me at reading people..."

In contrast to Shiro's muttering, Sora spoke proudly.

"Applying it to games is completely different from real-life socialization."

In a manner of speaking, girls—no, *people*...yes. Girls were like a visual novel where you had to make tens of thousands of timed choices every second. How could it be other than self-evident that such a game was ridiculous and impossible?

—But that was beside the point right now.

"Got it!..."

Sora had finally learned to read Immanity with the help of his sister. He checked that he had managed to read the whole volume. And closed the hardcover book with a thud. Then his face went serious as he joined his hands in front of his face.

"So—Shiro."

"...Mm."

"You've realized already, right?"

"...Yeah."

The siblings exchanged dialogue that only made sense to them.

"—What do you think?" the brother asked with an uncharacteristic lack of conviction. But Shiro just closed her eyes.

"I'll...follow you."

Opening her eyes just a little, with her typical lack of expression, she spoke in a monotone.

"...*Just as I promised*—anywhere."

—A *promise*.

His dad's new wife had brought him a *sister*—Shiro. The sister who was born too smart. And the brother who was born too dumb. Askew, they fit each other as siblings better than real siblings ever could. And when they came to be abandoned even by their parents, devoid of friends or allies, they exchanged a certain promise.—The sister who was too good and so couldn't understand people.—The brother who was too bad and so read people's expressions too deeply. Considering their complementary nature, the then-ten-year-old *brother* made a proposal. The three-year-old and already multilingual *sister* nodded and pinky-promised.

He rubbed that *sister's* head. It had been eight years since the sister had said that she would deign to follow him—Shiro. The brother who had never ended up taking her out of the room—Sora. If you asked if they had any regrets...

"Well—maybe I can take you someplace more fun than *that* world?"

Looking at the chess pieces visible beyond the distant horizon, Sora extracted his phone and started his task scheduler.

■■■

Steph fixed her gaze on the bubbling, hot water. It was important to pay attention not only to the time to steep the leaves, but also to the temperature of the water to put them in. The pancakes she had made the previous day would accompany it. The pancakes didn't really have the sugar they needed for tea, since humans had long since lost the land where it was grown. However, she compensated using cinnamon and other spices. She was quite proud of her work.

—Putting the tea set and the dainty plates of cut pancakes on a tray.

"...All right, I think this should be good."

Wiping her brow at the sense of accomplishment at a job well done.

"Excuse me, Miss?"

The maids interjected as if they had been waiting long for the right timing.

"Oh, what is it?"

"Ah, well... Please excuse my impertinence, but is something wrong, Miss?"

"…Impertinent, indeed. What's this all of a sudden?"

"Well, it's just… If you had asked, we, the staff, certainly would have prepared tea and sweets for you, yet you went ahead and steeped your own without a word… And with so much effort…"

——………Huh? Come to think of it, why should I have to steep my own tea? Faced with this question, Steph saw a certain image in her mind's eye.

"Oh! This is delicious. I didn't know you were so good around the house, Steph."

It was Sora, with a smile on his face and a teacup in his hand.

——……*Flush.* The feeling of blood rising to her cheeks.

"——Aaaaaaah, Goooooood!!"

Steph screamed and bashed her head against the wall.

"Why do I have to show off how good I am around the house with my homemade sweets! A man like that deserves nothing but water— with some rocks and grass as a side!"

"M-Miss! Please compose yourself!!"

"M-Missus! M-Miss Stephanie has—Miss Stephanie has lost her—"

The maids fell into chaos as they tried to stop Steph's forehead's resounding against the wall, the sound of the impacts loud and dull.

■■■

"*Hhh…*"

Sighing, Steph carried a silver tray down the hall. On the tray were a tea set and sweets for two—that is, the siblings. In the end, she couldn't win against her emotions and ended up bringing what she had prepared, and that made her sigh again. She hated herself, and yet, when she imagined being told it was delicious—

"…I can't deny part of me is looking forward to it… *Hh…*"

However. Steph froze in place.

"Wait a minute, Stephanie. Is this a taste that will appeal to otherworlders?"

Steph did have confidence in her own tea and baking skills. But her guests were *from another world*.

"Oh—cra—"

Another image crossed her mind.

"Egh, sorry, I gotta pass on this."

Sora, with a face.

"Aaahh… Th-that's no good; then I won't be able to get out by saying it was the maids—wait, why do I need an out? I don't even care what—yes, I do! Aahh, God… This is a curse…"

Already too frazzled to see straight. Steph breathed deeply and assembled an excuse in service of collecting her thoughts.

"Th-that's right. They've already belittled me to no end; should they now think I'm not capable of preparing some simple tea and sweets, it will bring shame upon the house of Dola. There is no mistaking that this is delicious; if it suits them not, it is a difference in culture—and certainly not—uh…"

Muttering excuses with her hands full. Steph struggled to open the door of her library and came back in.

"—What's this?"

—But, wherever she looked, the siblings had disappeared. She looked around and saw that on the *second floor* of the room, above the stairs, the door to the veranda had been opened, and the curtains swayed in the wind.

Steph went out onto the veranda…and there they were. The brother, in his butler outfit, was leaning over the rail of the veranda, capturing the city with his phone. The sister, a white-haired vision of a young lady—was leaning against her brother's legs, reading a book.

They seemed so natural as two in one, as though they would perish if split apart. At the too-picturesque sight of their relationship, Steph felt a significant constriction in her chest, while telling herself it was just nerves.

"…The town's excited."

Sora spoke to her, watching the commotion outside.

"—Yes...it is. After all, the gambling tournament to decide the monarch is still underway."

She placed the tray on the veranda table and poured tea into the cups.

"...So...here's tea."

"Oh, thanks."

"For the little sister as well."

"...Mm."

Sora took a swig of tea and looked back out on the city.

His first impression—the town of a "typical fantasy world"—had been a little bit off.

—Perhaps it was because the town had never been destroyed since war was forbidden. Several styles of architecture intermingled, reminiscent of Roman, classical, Baroque. The streets were paved, yet what traveled on them were carriages, and in the distant port floated three-masted sailing vessels. It appeared that not even the steam engine had been invented. The terraced fields built on the hills, visible in the distance, were being cultivated with methods even older than the mode of the city.

—Here was the recoil from not waging war. War had the ironic effect of accelerating *science*, pushing technology for fertilizer and fuel forward. Thinking back, Sora realized the books he had viewed in Steph's library were, almost without exception, handwritten and hand-copied. Printing either had not been invented or was not yet widely available.

"The Europe of the mid-Renaissance. Before the sky was sullied by the Industrial Revolution... A beautiful town."

"...Nice...strategy game...quote."

—But then, Sora thought, according to myth, the Great War that had reduced the planet to scorched earth hadn't happened only thousands of years ago. It was said that it had been thousands of years *already* by the time the Covenants were exchanged. Immanity couldn't use magic at all. In other words, humans labored under conditions equivalent to those in the world where they used to be.

After thousands of years, they were still at the level of their world in the early fifteenth century.

—In that case, what about the races who could use cheats like magic? What in the world were their civilizations like?

Then it occurred to Sora:

"Hey, Steph—why did you wanna be queen?"

"—Excuse me?"

"Well, I heard a rumor you were desperate because you weren't gonna be royalty anymore."

He recited what he'd heard outside the tavern-inn. But.

"—I don't really care about that."

—Rumors were rumors, after all. To be dismissed with a laugh. She came beside Sora, leaned from the veranda, and looked out at the town.

"…This nation, Elkia—it used to actually be a pretty big country, you know?"

She spoke with eyes that seemed to be looking into the distance— into the past.

"Long ago, there were several Immanity nations in the world. It was the biggest."

With a hint of pride, but also irony, she continued.

"Big enough to be the *last nation* of Immanity after it lost and lost, ever since the Ten Covenants…"

"……"

"It might look to you like we're a happy, bustling place. But no… Elkia has declined."

Once more looking out at the commotion of the town, but this time with sad eyes. Following her gaze, Sora found that he could imagine.

Territory lost. Surplus population on insufficient land. Shortages of resources and food leading to a deadlocked economy. Without land for food, there could be no production, and without production, there could be no jobs. The Ten Covenants may have secured peace—

—but then he remembered. The bandits who had attacked them as soon as they arrived in this world. The brother looked steadily in the direction of the cliff. His sister, who had been leaning on his legs reading a book, turned to Steph.

"It's true the old king—my grandfather—lost repeatedly in the play for dominion until we were backed into the capital with nothing else left. But Immanity had already been beaten to the ground, left poor as dirt..."

Gripping the railing, Steph spoke as if grinding her teeth.

"My grandfather was reviled as a fool king, yet he went on trying to save the country. He wasn't wrong—"

—If they didn't take back their land, humans wouldn't have long, anyway. Rather than sit and wait for destruction, he chose to charge forward for a chance at salvation—something like that.

"I—wanted to save Elkia..."

And then Steph seemed to be fighting back tears.

"And I wanted *to prove that my grandfather wasn't wrong.* I wanted to prove that for Immanity to live...we need to *take back* our territory, even if it means going on the offensive, or it won't be long before we really are gone."

—At Steph's words, wrung from her gloomy expression, Shiro asked a question with her usual look of indifference.

"...Steph...this country, this world...do you like it?"

"Yes—of course!"

—With a smile mixed with tears, Steph answered without hesitation. But the siblings lowered their heads instead.

"...Sounds nice..."

"...Yeah, I really envy you being able to say that with conviction."

But—the brother continued in a quiet but implacable voice and *cut down Stephanie Dola's hope.*

"But your wish won't come true."

"—Wha..."

"I'm also sorry to say—"

He rained a second blow upon the speechless Steph.

"Your grandfather—*ended his life as the worst fool king of all time, no matter how you look at it.*"

—.........

Breaking a terribly long silence, Steph opened her mouth as if squeezing it out.

"—What makes you…say that?"

Biting her lip and feeling her nails stabbing her clenched fists… If violence were not forbidden in this world, her palm would likely have flown to Sora's cheek, but instead she spun her certain anger into words. Because she loved him—no, *because she had been made to love him*, it was that much more difficult to tolerate this insult from him. However, in response to her question, Sora only sighed and scrolled through the photos he'd taken on his phone. A town reminiscent of fifteenth-century Europe. A beautiful town where new and old architecture intermingled thanks to a lack of war. But that was why it was so sad.

"At this rate—this country will die. *At the same time as the next monarch is chosen.*"

Words she hadn't anticipated all sent Steph not into confusion, but almost into hysteria as she rebutted.

"Wh-what do you mean! The very purpose of the tournament is—"

With an air of disbelief, Sora and Shiro looked up above their heads. A sky that wasn't gray like the one they knew, but blue as if primary-color ink had been spilled all over it.

—And they thought back to when they came to this world. To what "God" said. *Disboard*, the world on a board, where everything was decided by simple games. The world—

—We dreamed of.

—In which we've been—*reborn*.

"Steph, how long is this gambling tournament?"

Steph looked dissatisfied that she'd still not received a proper answer, but she replied anyway. "—Today is the last day."

Turning her gaze east from the veranda, to the place that looked like a castle.

"In the evening, the final match will be held in the royal hall. If no one raises any objections, the winner will become the new monarch…What of it?"

—*Whump.* The sister closed her book and stood up. The brother stretched dramatically and slapped his cheeks.

"—Hmp! Hey, little sister."

"…Mm."

"Will you follow your brother no matter what?"

"Yeah."

"Wow, that was quick. I mean, I've got to prepare myself, too—"

"…B.S."

"Hnh?"

"…You look like you're having…fun."

She was expressionless, as usual. But there was the hint of a smile only her brother could see.

"—Ha-ha, I can't fool you, eh?"

At this, the two turned and walked back.

"Wai—wh-where are you going?!"

"The royal castle."

"—Hunh?"

Unable to grasp the intent behind Sora's prompt answer, Steph uttered a silly sound. But they took no notice and went on.

"We'll go prove your grandfather was right."

"——Wha?"

Feeling the presence of Steph hurriedly catching up behind him. Sora checked what he'd put into the task scheduler on his phone.

—*Objective—Try being king, for now.* Sora chuckled, put his phone back in his pocket, and spoke.

"After we managed to get reborn into this world, it would suck if we ended up without a place to live."

Shiro nodded in agreement.

"Think I'll go become king and take back some territory."

—Had she heard him right? Stephanie Dola carefully reviewed the words she had heard. Once she was sure that she couldn't have misheard him, she looked at his back. He had a bounce in his step as if he were just going down the street for some groceries. But it was full of brazen pride and confidence, like he was going to check something that was already settled—the back of the man who had declared he would reclaim the territory of the human race.

"Oh, that's right."

Sora grabbed the sweet that had been left on the table of the veranda and stuffed it in his mouth.

"—Oh."

With Steph looking like she'd forgotten herself, Sora spoke.

"Mm, this is good. The tea and the sweets were both really good. Thanks."

Sora turned to say these words with a smile. Was it, after all, the Covenants that made her heart race? Steph hardly knew anymore.

⏻ CHAPTER 3
EXPERT

Evening—Great Hall, Elkia Royal Castle.

There, where it appeared that the final match to decide the monarch had ended, in front of the throne, were a small table and a pair of chairs. One person sat there, surrounded by a crowd that packed the hall.

—Sitting at the table, with folded arms and a blank expression, with black clothes and a black veil as if for a funeral, with an emptiness about her that somehow suggested a corpse, was a girl with long black hair. Yes…it was that girl—the one who'd cheated to eliminate Steph at the tavern.

An old man wrapped in official-looking garb spoke.

"—This woman, Chlammy Zell, has in the end emerged victorious in the battle to decide the crown… Is there anyone left who would challenge her?"

The hall only murmured. It seemed there was no one who would challenge her. It was as expected—for Chalmmy had so far won every match she fought. At this point there could be no one who expected to defeat her. Chlammy, closing her eyes upon these facts and casting a still deeper emotionless shadow over her expression-less face. Seeing this, the old man continued.

"—Then, in accordance with the will of the late king—I shall crown Chlammy as the new Queen of Elkia. If there be anyone among you who may object, speak now; if not, your silence shall—"

"Oh, yeah, here! Objection! Objection!"

At that voice which rang out to interrupt the speech, the black-haired girl's—Chlammy's—eyes opened. The eyes of the stirring crowd all turned at once to the source of the voice. And there stood a butler and a girl with long, white hair—Sora and Shiro, raising their hands.

"Right, right. We have an objection, we two."

"...Mm."

"...Who are you?"

Chlammy looked at them expressionlessly, then moved her eyes behind them.

"—Servants of Stephanie Dola?"

Behind the two, Steph's shoulders jolted. And, emotionlessly, but with a trace of ridicule, Chlammy spoke.

"...You disqualified yourself by losing to me, and now you send your servants? Truly, your inability to accept defeat is unsightly..." Chlammy said, making no attempt to conceal her scorn. But Sora stepped up lightly and replied:

"—Aha-ha, you're in no place to talk about that, are you?"

"—Whatever do you mean?"

"Well, you know, really, I'm not that interested in the royal throne and such; it seems like it would be a drag."

As Sora spoke, scratching his head, looking like he really thought it was a drag, Chlammy squinted.

"...Then would you please leave my sight? This is no place to bring children to play."

Sora smiled and continued. "But, you know," he said, sharpening his gaze.

"It's no place to give the throne to a *charlatan backed by another country* either, now, is it?"

This line made a stir in the castle.

—Another country?—What's this about? Ignoring such voices, Sora asked so only Shiro could hear.

"—You find 'em?"

In Shiro's hand was the phone Sora had used the previous day to capture the tavern. Shiro answered with the number of people who were in the photos displayed on the screen *and also in this hall*.

"…Four."

"How many of them have their ears hidden?"

"…One."

"Bingo. Point in sync with me."

"…Mm."

As the siblings plotted, Steph spoke up.

"Hey—wh-what's this about another country?"

Steph whispered this to Sora, who answered disgustedly.

"You still don't get it? Okay, hypothetically, all right? Hypothetically—"
And then, loudly:

"*Hypothetically, if someone who won using magic by colluding with an Elf* were to become the monarch, this country would be screwed, right?"

The din in the castle finally began to take on a note of fear. As Sora watched, he wondered, Hadn't anyone figured it out?

"…Well, if no one can catch on to such a glaring flaw, it's only natural that humans would get their asses kicked."

"—You there."

…Quietly standing up, Chlammy walked toward Sora. With a face from which feeling was obscured even further by the veil, and with a strangely intimidating presence.

"Are you trying to say that I'm using magic to cheat?"

"Oh, my. Didn't you hear me say 'hypothetically'? Or did I hit a nerve?"

But it was as if he didn't even feel her presence. Brushing it off like a leaf, Sora's provocation was clear. But he must have had absolute confidence.

"—Very well. If you object, then I shall certainly give you your game!"

"Thaaanks! I'd sure appreciate it! But—"

As Chlammy tried to take out her cards, Sora cut her off.

"If you want to play poker—*it would be better if you got rid of your partner over there.*"

As Sora said this with a smile, Shiro took his cue and pointed. The din quieted like a wave that had broken, and all eyes turned in that direction. Chlammy and the man pointed to slightly tensed their faces at the same time. That little change was more than enough to show Sora that he was dead-on.

"Whatever are you talking about?"

"Oh, really? Then will someone take off that guy's hat?"

The man pointed to took a step back, but the crowd around him slowly drew off his hat. Two ears popped out.

—The kind you always see in fantasy—that's right, the long ears of an Elf.

It-it's an Elf!

The crowd murmured.

Hey, wait…what if that guy's actually right—

The crowd murmured more loudly.

That bitch, she was cheating with magic?!

"Oh, my dear cool-beauty-wannabe charlatan, aren't you going to *save your friend?*"

Though Sora teased her, Chlammy did not change her expression.

"—How many times must I tell you? I have no idea what you speak of."

"Oh, okay. So we can kick him out, no problem, right?"

Sora beamed and flicked his hand a couple of times so as to dismiss the man to the outside. And, once again, he faced Chlammy and pulled out another phone—Shiro's phone.

"All right, you ready for some poker?"

Launching an app or two on the phone, Sora played around with a smile.

—A few seconds of silence. Then Chlammy, still expressionless, closed her eyes and spoke.

"—I see you found an Elf to collude with to put me up as a magic-using enemy of the human race…is that it?"

"Huh, you think up some pretty good excuses. Or did you have it reserved?"

Though Sora continued with his provocations, Chlammy kept speaking.

"—But if that's how you want to play, I have my pride."

Still letting no expression through, while staring daggers through her veil, through Sora.

"Please go ahead and send that Elf wherever you like. And then—let us play a game ideal for demonstrating true skill, with no part for cheating to play."

But Sora grinned back as if her stare, her proposal were just what he was expecting.

"That's fine. Fifth of the Ten Covenants: *'The party challenged shall have the right to determine the game'*—eh, I won't ask why you declined to play poker, though. I'm such a nice guy. ♥"

Sora turned his phone camera to Chlammy and snapped a picture.

"Hmm, you're not very photogenic, you know? You'd really look cuter if you smiled a little more."

And he showed her the picture on his screen. Chlammy's piercing stare was met by Sora's eyes as if peering in.

—Those eyes, peering in as if seeing through everything. Chlammy felt a slight chill—.

Chlammy, having said she'd go home and get *a game ideal for demonstrating true skill* or something, said to wait a bit and left the castle. Sora and company, for their part, decided to wait in the sunset of the castle courtyard. As Sora and Shiro sat on a bench and waited, playing with their phones, Steph looked about. Checking that no one was around, and then posing a question to Sora as if she'd been waiting forever.

"—D-does that mean she used magic on me?!"

"…Hey—you're too loud!"

Steph didn't seem to get why they had moved.

—But it did seem she had finally grasped the truth of the cheating that had defeated her. Especially knowing that the cheating was based on magic, her feelings were understandable. But Sora thought of something else and answered absently.

"Yeah, that's right… To be precise, that Elf of hers did, I guess."

"Wh-what kind of magic?"

What kind of magic had they used? And how could Sora, a mere human, have seen through it? Another question was that thing they were using. Some tool from their world—could it detect magic? Steph waited for the answer with expectant eyes, but what came back—

"Who knows? I sure don't."

—betrayed her expectations entirely. Ignoring Steph as she gaped speechless, Sora answered calmly.

"There's no question she's cheating. In the tavern, we saw her playing you, but the composition of her hands was obviously nonrandom. Shiro and I both noticed right away."

"…Shiro noticed."

"You're such a stickler, my sister…well, whatever."

—The day before, at the tavern on the first floor of the inn. Inside Steph and Chlammy had played poker, and outside Sora had cheated while playing the very same game of poker; the pronouncement he'd made on the matter had been absolute. But—

"But there's no way I could figure out how she's doing it. I don't know anything about magic."

"………"

Sora answered indifferently as Steph froze with her mouth half open.

"Man, that magic is something. If they're altering your memory or reprinting the face-down cards or something, there's no way you can prove that; hell, there's no way you can win. If humans can't detect it, then you ain't gonna discover it."

"——Wai—"

Steph, apparently finally recovered from paralysis, shook her head, and interrogated him.

"Wait a minute, then how are you supposed to win!"

"Huh? You can't win."

Sora responded casually and decisively as Steph stood speechless once again.

"Who's gonna face that? That's certain failure—you don't even have a one-in-a-million chance to win."

But, before Steph recovered again and started shouting, he added further.

"Duh, that's why *we avoided that.*"

"—Huh?"

Sora shifted his posture to face Steph directly and spoke.

"Okay, I'm gonna make this as simple as possible, all right?"

"V-very well..."

"First of all, this is a free-for-all tournament to decide the monarch. Whoever wins will be the representative of Immanity."

"Yes..."

"But the plan is flawed. *Because it leaves room for other countries to intervene.*"

"—Yes. I suppose, so..."

Steph averted her eyes, chagrined she'd not realized this on her own until it was pointed out.

—Indeed, with the system of an unconditional free-for-all tournament, human-undetectable cheating could be used, *by another country, to let someone win and form a puppet government.* Humans were then doomed to fail in the running and to die as a race. The plan was full of holes. The epitome of foolishness.

"—So, this isn't a battle of individuals. It's a battle of *countries*, of *diplomacy.* Got it?"

"Uh, yes...I take your meaning."

"Now, these...Elves, right? They're trying to take advantage of this to install a puppet monarch—but surely you don't think that the Elves are the only ones who would think of this?"

"—W-well…"

"Surely other countries have thought of it. Whether they've carried it out or not, it's very likely."

Which meant—.

"We just have to take advantage of that and make them think *we're one of them.*"

Playing with his phone in his hand, Sora smiled mischievously.

"Now that we've shown her a device she didn't figure the humans had *and made her think that we saw through the Elf's magic with it*, she'll be shouldered with the risk that if she uses obvious magic, we'll expose and disqualify her right away. Plus, we cast doubt on the actual user and drove him out—"

"In—in that case—we can expect a match with no cheating!"

Steph's face lit up, but Sora dropped his shoulders with a look of disgust.

"—For God's sake, how mushy is your brain?"

"Wh-why am I being censured?!"

"Weren't you listening? I said the idea that another country might intervene is *conceivable*. Which means we can assume that *they've already taken the possibility of people like us into account.*"

"Oh……"

Then Sora brought his thoughts back to their original line and considered.

"—The enemy must have one ready. You know, a *cheat that will put them ahead even in this situation.*"

…And then Steph's words rang in Sora's mind.

"Steph, you said Immanity can't use magic, but it can use games that use magic, right?"

"Uh, yes…"

Hmm…Sora's face cleared as if the answer to his ruminations had appeared.

"You said Elf is best at magic, right? Then they must have anticipated a challenge from a country with the technology to detect magic and prepared a game with more complicated, hard-to-reveal cheat magic—that's probably what they went to get."

But Steph's face clouded at these words.

"Th-that's... Doesn't that make things even worse?"

"—What? What do you mean?"

"Huh? I mean, if they're using more complicated, hard-to-reveal cheating magic—"

Sora sighed for the umpteenth time today.

"Look here—for pure, mere humans like us, *the greatest threat is simple magic, like if they were to mess with us directly by altering our memories or viewing our vision.* 'Cause we wouldn't know. But, if their game is assuming *they're playing a country to whom that doesn't apply,* they can't do that."

In other words, the game would look fair *on the surface.* But hide a mechanism that would give them an overwhelming advantage. And it would be unperceivable—which meant that they wouldn't mess with them directly. Certainly, they'd hide an *overwhelmingly advantageous cheat.* But it wouldn't be an unbeatable cheat like what they used for the poker game with Steph. *A bluff to make them bring out that game: That was what the phone was for.* So far, everything was going well.

"B-but..."

Steph, seeming to have finally gotten it, gave an on-the-mark opinion for the first time.

"Even so—doesn't that mean we'll still be at an overwhelming disadvantage?"

"Sure it does. *Is there a problem with that?*"

But Sora responded calmly, drawing close to Shiro, who was sitting on the bench.

"As long as the game is *possible to win in principle,* 'lose' isn't in Blank's dictionary."

"...Mm."

Shiro nodded in agreement, having just shut out a shogi app on the highest difficulty.

—Then...Shiro turned, responding to something. The shadow that approached—it took a while to realize that it was Chlammy.

"...Oh, crap, you don't think she heard us?"

Sora muttered in a voice only Shiro could hear, and Shiro nodded, as if to say, It's okay. Then Chlammy's first words backed it up.

"—Let me ask you straight-out. *Whose spies* are you?"

Sora sighed in relief inside. But, instead of showing it, he grinned.

"Oh, you see, we're actually from that country—ha, you think we'd answer? Are you stupid?"

"—I won't give you this country."

"I'm quite aware of that, ma'am. After all, yooouuu wanna give it to the Elllves, right?"

"…No."

Though Sora continued his grinning provocation, Chlammy put it down with stern eyes.

"I won't give it to anyone. Our country belongs to us."

"——Hmmm?"

To Sora's *My, I didn't expect that* prompt, Chlammy declared firmly:

"I took Elf's help in order to guarantee humans a place to live—I'm sure you can't imagine the complexity of the contracts I exchanged for this… As soon as we've secured the minimum territory we need—I will break with Elf."

—Holy crap… The urge to clutch his head in frustration was too great even for Sora to resist. Letting out a sincerely pained chuckle, he said:

"You're telling this plan to someone who might be a spy for another country? Are you stupid? Do you want to die?"

But Chlammy glared at Sora with eyes full of confidence that could be seen even through the veil.

"… Regardless of what country you're spying for, there's no chance you can beat me."

"—Hmmm, that's some confidence you've got there."

"It's just a fact. The magic of the world's largest country, Elven Gard—the magic of the Elves—cannot be overcome by any race. That's why, if you face this one greatest country head-on, you lose. There are no exceptions."

…Hm.

"…If you still consider yourself Immanity—"

Chlammy, softening her stern gaze, looking into Sora's eyes.

"If you still feel anything for this country, for Immanity, I want you to give up your spying and forfeit this match. I swear I will not allow the Elves to make me their puppet."

"…"

As Sora quietly took in her words, she came to the brink of pleading.

"—We can't use magic, or even detect it—that's us, Immanity."

From the expression hidden under the black veil, Chlammy let through a shade of anguish.

"For us to survive in this world, we must obtain the right to live under the protection of a great country, and then abandon all contests and close ourselves off entirely—this is the only way. Surely you see?"

…Hm. According to the Ten Covenants, the party challenged had the right to determine the game. Indeed, if they were to accept the help of the most powerful race and obtain a certain domain, refusing all contests and isolating themselves would be an efficient and effective strategy. In exchange for gaining nothing, they would lose nothing. It was like how, in shogi, *the most powerful formation is one that doesn't move.* But, on the other hand—

"…Hmm, I see… Not a bad plan. I see what you're saying…"

"Then you will forfeit this match for me…"

As Chlammy closed her eyes gratefully—

"But I refuse."

Sora responded with words that opened her eyes up.

"—May I…hear your reasoning?"

"Heh-heh, it's like this…"

Sora, drawing in his sister, who until now had been watching the proceedings from the side with a face betraying no emotion.

"One of Blank's favorite things—

""—is saying *No* to someone who thinks
she has an overwhelming advantage…!""

Shiro joined with Sora's line in harmony. At this statement, which was totally bizarre to Chlammy and Steph, who didn't know the *reference*, the two could only stare speechless at the jubilant siblings.

"Bwa-ha-ha! Number Four on my list of lines I wanted to try saying sometime—I got to say it in real life!"

"…Brother, mad props."

As the siblings gave each other thumbs-up, Chlammy's shoulders shook. Perhaps she took it as a provocation, or a sign that there was no room for negotiation.

"—I wasted my time talking to you. As you wish, I shall twist you down by force… I'll be waiting in the hall."

"Sure, sure. Make sure you bring that *power you got by selling someone else your ass.*"

Sora watched Chlammy off, making a point of choosing the words to irritate her.

"I-is that okay? I thought she did have a point…"

Steph asked the question hesitantly, and Sora looked at her dumbfounded.

"—Please, don't you think it's about time you learned to doubt people?"

Sora counted up fingers.

"One, *just where's the evidence that anything she said was true?*"

"Oh…"

While Steph looked down as if she couldn't deny the shame, Sora, heedless, carried on counting.

"Two, if she has a certain route to victory, then why did she come to try to talk us into forfeiting?"

"…Oh!"

Steph raised her face as if she couldn't miss this truth.

"There is a one-in-a-million chance she'll lose…so *she has no certain route to victory*?!"

So—it was just as Sora foresaw. Smiling at Steph's rare correct answer, Sora raised his third and fourth fingers.

"Three, if it is all true, we can't trust the human race to an idiot who would reveal all that to someone she suspects is a foreign spy. And, four, if we let her see our hand, we're finished. Got it?"

Steph opened her mouth dumbly and nodded repeatedly.

"Y-you put all that thought into that line…"

…Never suspecting that it was a reference. Steph, sincerely reevaluating Sora, realized heat was rising to her face and shook it off as Sora cast his eyes to the direction Chlammy went—the path that led to the castle hall.

"…Well, that's not all it's about. She's—well, you are, too, but—"

He turned his gaze to Shiro. Shiro nodded and they walked together.

"—kind of underestimating us people."

■■■

The group returned to the hall. What they saw was a huge crowd filling it, as if they had been waiting forever. And, indeed, set up in front of the throne, a small table and a pair of chairs. And, on the table—

"A chessboard…?"

This time it was Sora's turn to be confused. A game hiding Elf magic… He had considered many possible games—but he hadn't expected chess. Because—just how were you supposed to cheat at chess? Sora found himself unable to wipe away misgivings, this having had gone over and to the side of his expectations. Still, Chlammy set in the opposing chair, explaining in a voice without emotion.

"That's right, it's chess. However—it's not just chess."

With that, she took out a small box and dumped the pieces on the board.

—And then the thirty-two pieces, sixteen each for white and black, slid across the board on their own, taking their positions. As if—yes—

"That's right, it's chess in which the pieces have will…"

Chlammy, answering as if she had read Sora's thoughts.

"The pieces move automatically. All you have to do is command. And they will move as you command."

"……I see. That's how it is."

—Now, this was an annoying game. Sora thought through all the cheats that seemed likely and clucked.

"…What now, Shiro?"

If it were normal chess, Shiro would *win unconditionally*. But only if it were normal chess. Moreover, it was certain that the opponent had hidden some kind of magic to cheat.

"…Don't worry… I won't lose at chess."

Shiro boldly stepped forward.

—But, first, Sora checked.

"Hey, we can switch in the middle, right?"

""—?""

Both Chlammy and Shiro looked doubtful.

"Sorry, but we're a two-in-one player. Plus, it seems that you're the only one who knows all about this game, right? Down to its *nooks and crannies*, you know what I mean?"

Sora talked while he futzed with his phone in his hand. Chlammy peered into Sora's eyes as if to assess his intention. But Sora's eyes shed no light on anything.

—Anyone that dumb wouldn't be able to hold up half of " ".

"—As you like."

Whether she was concerned about the phone in Sora's hand or wary that she'd not been able to read anything. Chlammy spoke as if spitting—but.

"…Brother, you think I'm going to lose…?"

Unexpectedly, the one who raised an argument—was one who was supposed to hold up the other half, his sister.

"Shiro, don't get too heated. If this were normal chess, there's not a one-in-a-million chance you'd lose."

"…Mm."

Shiro nodded as if this was obvious. And Sora meant it from his heart. There's no way she'd lose.

—But.

"This *isn't normal chess*—even more so than she's told us."

"……"

"Don't forget. We're two in one; together, we are the best. Okay?"

"…I'm sorry. I'll be careful…"

"Super! Now go give 'em hell!"

With that, he stroked Shiro's head—and said in a whisper at her ear.

"—I'll figure out what her cheat is and how to counter it. Meanwhile, you *kick her ass.*"

Shiro nodded once and slowly sat down at the table. Since the seat was a bit too low for young Shiro, she sat on her heels on top of it, in the traditional *seiza* floor-sitting style.

"Are you done talking?—In that case, let's begin; *you may make the first move.*"

"…—"

Shiro's brow twitched at the obvious provocation.

To Shiro, who dismissed chess as "just like tic-tac-toe," this was equivalent to Chlammy saying she would *let her win.* Because chess, in principle, is a game in which the player who goes first will always win as long as she keeps making the best moves. The player who goes second can only draw if her opponent makes at least one mistake.

"Pawn b2 to b4."

The words of Shiro, slightly soured, began the game. The chessboard on which the pieces moved not in the players' hands, but on their own in response to spoken commands. The pawn moved two spaces forward, as the rules permitted only on its first move.

—But Chlammy had said that the pieces had will. It couldn't be just that they moved on their own—. Heedless of Sora's such contemplation, Chlammy murmured quietly.

"Pawn Seven, *forward.*"

The next moment—the pawn that had been named—

——moved *three spaces forward*.

""""—Whaa?!""""

Sora exclaimed as the crowd resounded with a murmur.

"The *pieces have will*—didn't I tell you?"

Chlammy formed a thin grin and explained.

"The pieces move in response to a player's *charisma*, *authority*, *leadership*...reflecting her *qualifications as a monarch*—don't you think it's a game well suited to decide the actual monarch?"

"—*Tsk!*"

Sora clucked his toungue—but remained unperturbed...

"...Pawn d2 to d3."

...Shiro played on calmly, straightforwardly.

"Oh, is that all? You're taking your time, aren't you?"

...But, once Shiro got into a game, provocation was useless. One mustn't forget that though she had had help from her brother, her overwhelming concentration had *even beaten a god*.

......And. In fact.

Without agitation at Chlammy's continued seemingly illegal moves. And without any risks, Shiro continued to move her pieces—

"...No way."

This was mumbled by Steph, watching the match from beside Sora. But it must have been what everyone in the castle was thinking in their hearts. When Chlammy was moving her pieces in a manner nigh impossible to predict—. Just how was it *possible to start to corner her?* The hall filled with hubbub. Shiro responded to the pieces' outrageous movements with divine command. An inhuman calm that made one think, This is what it means to be clear as a lake.

"U-unbelievable... She's overpowering an opponent who's practically ignoring the rules?"

"Yeah."

However, Sora had a calm view of the situation himself.

"But that's nothing worth getting so worked up about."

"Huh?"

"It's like in shogi—well, I don't know if you have it in this world, but anyway. An elite player can play without rook, bishop, golds, silvers, knights, or lances—in other words, *just with king and pawns, and still shut their opponent down...* The difference between a master and an intermediate player isn't a gap that can be closed by breaking a few rules."

Having said that.

"—However."

There was still a *certain something* Sora feared. If, just as Chlammy had said, the key to this game was that the *pieces had will...* And then—his fear forthwith became reality.

"Pawn Five, forward."

Shiro's pawn, thus commanded—

—still *did not move.*

"...Uh?"

For the first time since the beginning of the match, confusion arose on Shiro's face. Steph looked likewise confused, but in contrast Sora was calm.

"—Yep, there it is."

Sora clucked as his prediction hit the mark. So. The key was that in this version of chess, the pieces could move disregarding the rules if you had charisma—but that wasn't it. It was that *if you didn't have enough charisma, the pieces wouldn't move.* A strategy that wouldn't normally work if the pieces were real soldiers—namely:

"So, *you can't sacrifice.*"

—No soldier normally would gladly die for everyone. It was a maneuver that only became possible with a thorough structure and system of command—or by morale equivalent to insanity. And, if the avenue of "sacrifice" was closed off—

"___"

Shiro bit her nails and began to think long for the first time.

...Yes—this would greatly limit future tactics. However, the soldiers of the thinly smiling Chlammy kept moving, in perfect order.

...Though Shiro had been on top, it did not take long for her to begin to be cornered.

—The situation had worsened in a flash. Their morale lost, the pieces ignored her commands yet further, and Shiro began to grow irritable. With the commander's irritation relaying itself to the troops, a vicious circle formed—.

...In such a situation, there could be no hope.

"...!"

It must have hit her—her chance to win had vanished.

But—*it was enough.* Shiro had kept up the match as she allowed Sora to focus on observing. Dead eyes, full of self-derision—*no matter how you looked at it, she had no charisma.* The movements of Chlammy's pieces were more than enough to tell him the truth behind the cheating.

—Sora put his hand on his sister's head and spoke.

"Shiro, my turn."

"......"

His sister's eyes could not be seen beyond the long, white hair over her sunken face. Yet it could be inferred that they contained traces of tears.

—It was only natural. " " couldn't have a loss. Especially not at chess, at which the sister had never lost once.

"......Brother...I'm sorry."

"—What's wrong?"

".........I...lost...I'm...sor...ry."

With that, Shiro put her face into her brother's chest. But Sora hugged her head and spoke.

"Huh? What are you talking about; we haven't lost yet."

"......"

"The two of us *together* make Blank—until I lose, we haven't lost."

Sora's words drew Shiro's eyes up. His face was full of his usual brazen confidence—that there was no way they could fail.

"And, besides, *this isn't chess*—when have you ever beat me at *this game*?"

"...Uh?"

"Aw, just watch—this game is *my territory.*"

Gwoosh, gwoosh. Sora rubbed the tears from the eyes of his sister, invisible behind her bangs. Her expression was hidden below her head, but it still appeared to be downcast. The sister made as

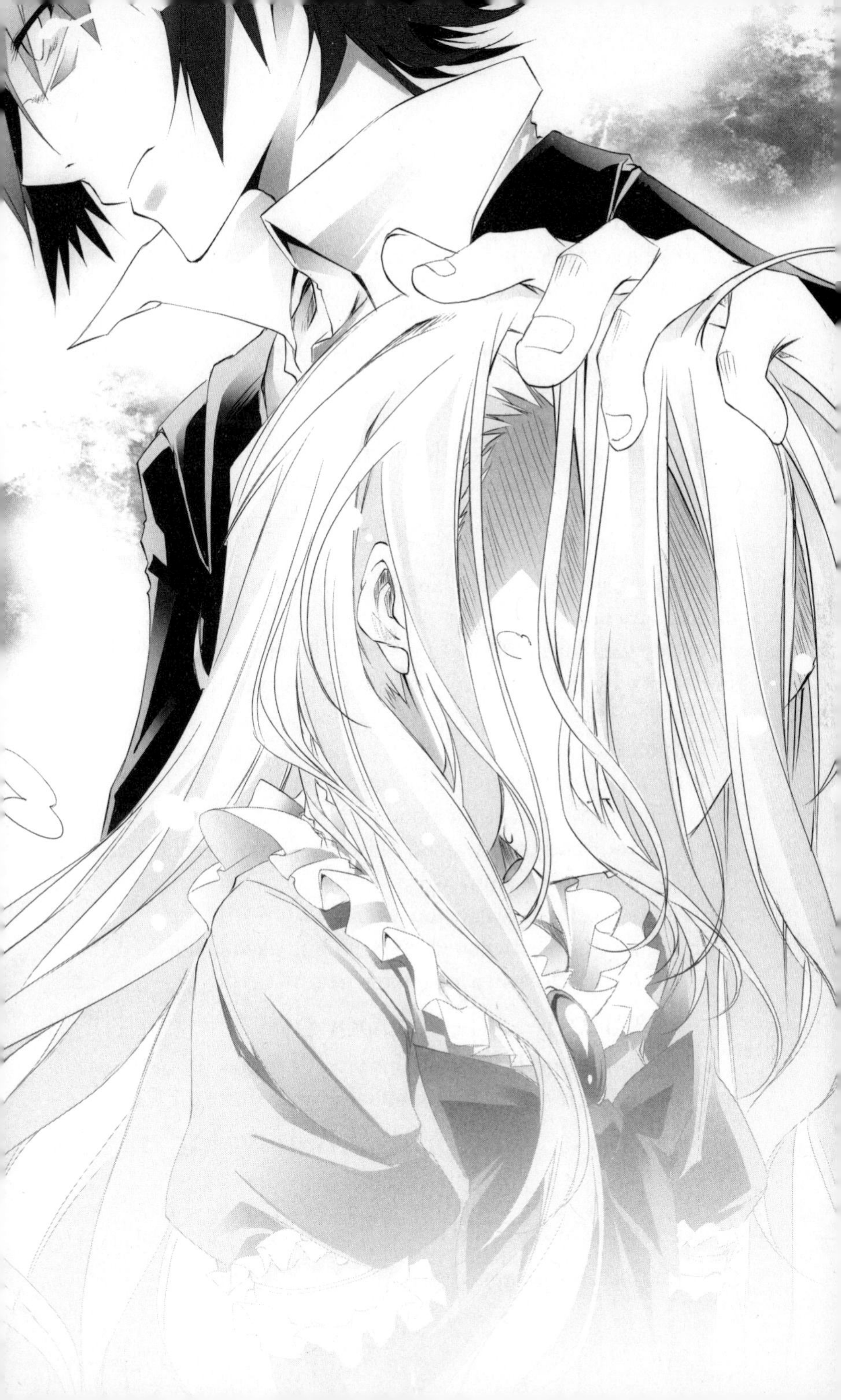

if to withdraw from the seat as she was guided—but then Sora stopped her.

"Such a crybaby. A little girl abandoning a game in the middle, and an easygoing brother who thinks he can catch up now... It looks like you two certainly do have the qualities of a monarch. *Albeit a very foolish one.*"

The words of Chlammy were disregarded. As Sora lifted up his sister, who was about to withdraw.

"...?!"

Shiro flinched at being suddenly lifted.

—Sora lifted up his sister, who was too light even for a girl of eleven. He then sat at the table and settled her on his lap.

"...?"

"Didn't I say the two of us are Blank? Stay here. And help me out if I lose my cool."

Sora opened his mouth heedless of his sister's blank stare. With a smile, yet with infinite creepiness, Sora put words to Chlammy.

Namely:

"Hey, bitch."

"—Could it be...that you mean to address me?"

"I'm gonna take you down along with those cheats you sold every orifice in your body to the good old Elves for, so you'd better start thinking how you're gonna word your apology—making my sister cry is gonna cost you dearly, you *whore.*"

Chlammy's cheek twitched slightly, but paying no heed. Sora faced the board. Drew in a long, long breath—and.

"Attention—all—troooops!"

To say nothing of the sister on his lap. All the people in the castle hall plugged their ears as Sora shouted so as to shake the walls.

"To those who prove their valor in this fight—

on my royal authority, *I shall grant the right*

to bang once the woman of your fancy!"

——. The castle was overtaken by a silence like the bottom of the sea. The meanings of the silence—doubt, contempt, disbelief. But Sora carried on all the same.

"Moreover! To those of you soldiers who fight on the front lines and emerge victorious, I shall exempt you from further military duty, and from taxes for the rest of your lives! I guarantee you a stipend from the national treasury! Therefore—virgins, die not! And those of you with families, with loved ones awaiting you—all of you men must come back alive!"

The unsurpassably vulgar speech cast a stiller silence over the castle.

——But. From the chessboard.

"Hoooooooooooooooo!!"

—Such a battle cry resounded. As if in an inverse proportion, the crowd cringed violently. But the speech was still not over.

"Men, soldiers! Heed well my words! This fight is for us—for Elkia, for humans! This fight will determine into whose hands falls this city, our last fortress—the fate of mankind hangs in the balance! Open your ears! Open your eyes; is it right——"

Pointing fiercely to his opponent—to Chlammy, he shouted.

"—to entrust the throne of this country to this corpselike, *soft-headed harlot!*"

"Wha—"

Ignoring the speechless Chlammy, he grabbed the morosely hanging head of his sister. He moved aside her bangs to show her face.

The long, white albino hair parted to reveal skin as white as snow and eyes as red as rubies, deep enough to suck you in—yet tinged with sadness.

"If we are victorious, she will be queen! Yes, she who just now— out of care for all of you!—hardened her heart to lead you to victory, and shed tears from that same heart when you rejected her orders as merciless! I shall ask but once—

"——do you yet call yourselves men?"

And, without pausing, he sent orders to a pawn.

"Tell the Seventh Pawn Company! The enemy encroaches from the front! If we hold our ground, we shall be trapped and flanked— *Rush on and take the rear!*—Seize the initiative!"

With this, as if carried along with his cry. The pawn moved forward two spaces, *and then went on behind the enemy pawn*—and smashed it.

"Wha—How could that—?!"

As Chlammy lost her composure, Sora smirked back broadly and spoke.

"What's this, what's this? It's just what you were doing; is there something strange about it?"

"—Hnck!"

On Sora's lap, however, his sister mumbled.

"…But, if this were a real war…with this, the troops would be worn out…couldn't move for a while."

"Yes, it's just as you say—Second Cavalry Squadron! Waste not the path to life the Seventh Pawn Company has carved! Protect the *heroes* who have carved this path with everything you have!"

And, *without waiting for his opponent to take her turn,* he fired off yet another notice.

"And, finally, the king and queen! Which means us, but anyway— get out there on the front!"

—This command, far-flung from the conventions of chess, opened not only the crowd's eyes, but even Shiro's. And that wasn't all.

"H-hey, hold on! What you think you're doing, skipping my—!"

—This objection from Chlammy was met by Sora with the eyes used to pity a stray dog.

"Huh? Are you stupid? In a real war, who the hell waits for his opponent's turn?"

To begin with, the pieces were moving. Which meant *his commands were accepted.*

"If you're worried about your turn, all you have to do is send commands faster than me, Miss Dunderhead. ♥"

Sora, shooting back at her as if to say, You got a problem, tell it to the chessboard. He pouring out sophistry like it was as easy as breathing. But—in fact, the pieces were moving. Which meant there was no foul. In which case—

"Nggk—Pawn Companies, advance in order! Build a wall!!"

Chlammy, hastily shooting off orders to fight back. Instantly, Sora *spun it against her.*

"Ah! Behold these heartless cowards who hide themselves behind a wall of men!"

Even mixing in flamboyant gestures, Sora's acting was that of a natural as he shouted on.

"What kind of king, what kind of queen, forces their soldiers to fight on the front while they sit back in the rear! A king, a queen—a ruler should be one who shows their people the way!—All of you, follow us, you proud knights, bishops, and rooks! Now is the time to show deeds worthy of your names! Support the pawns, and bring them to *promotion!*"

—Slandering his opponent's strategy, he exploited it to boost morale. His speech modeled after real-world propaganda rallied the pieces to move rapidly.

And once more he spoke to Chlammy—and, consequently, the pieces she led.

"Hm—using the Elves' magic to boost *your own army's morale*—in terms of a real war you might call it—*brainwashing?*"

"—!"

Chlammy's expression moved slightly. If she thought her slip-up wouldn't reveal that he was dead-on, she underestimated the man named Sora.

"I see. It's difficult to prove, yet overwhelmingly advantageous in the progress of this game. The more of a master your opponent is at chess, the less she'll be able to predict the movements of your pieces, and, unable to sacrifice her pieces, she'll be thrown into disarray..."

Putting his hand on his sister's head.

"However, you made a *big mistake.*"

Then he rang out with another speech.

"In all of history, since time immemorial, there has not been one case of a wise monarch who controlled their army through oppression; the truth is, people will only fight for what is right—and, *in this world, there is only one thing that is absolutely right!*"

His sister, whose eyes were usually listlessly half-closed. Now subjected to a series of events that made her eyes open wide. He showed that face—*with eyes fully open*, of a beautiful girl who enchanted everyone who saw her.

"Soldiers, you stand before your queen! If you call yourselves men, bring no more tears to these eyes!"

—As if in response. Once more from the board came a skin-shaking roar.

"—That's right... *Cute* is the sole absolute law of this world."

Embracing his sister on his lap, Sora said it boldly. The board alone echoed back, creating a chilling imbalance with the hall—but that was disregarded. For the people of this world, ignorant of war, could not know.

—The reason men put their lives on the line to fight was the same in any world. It was for those they loved. It was for the honor to attract those they loved. Put bluntly, without decoration:

—It was for *sexy time*...and that alone...

"!—Pawn Five! Smash the enemy knight!"

The pawn commanded by Chlammy moved to attack his knight—but Sora held his sister on one side, stood from his chair, waved his arm, and shouted:

"Honored knights, will you allow your knighthoods bestowed upon you by the grace of your queen to be overthrown by common infantry? In the name of your queen, and on your knighthood, I permit you not to die! You face mere footmen; they know no skill but backstabbing! Turn, step back, and hold the line—*clear a path by your sword and your shield!*"

With that, the pawn that should have been attacking not only failed to capture the knight—*but was pulverized just before it could.*

""—Whaaaaaaa?!""

Not just Chlammy, but also Steph, and in fact the whole castle cried out in surprise. Even so, it went unheard. Sora shouted on as if he were really standing on the battleground.

"Well you have withstood; well you have stood your ground, proud knight! This is what it means to be a sword of the people!— But now you may rest your sword for a time and enjoy your leave! I pledge on my name that those who achieve on this battlefield will be rewarded as they deserve!"

And so the knight—the mere piece. Turned to face Sora—no...his *king*. Tipped as to bow—and vanished from the board, moving to the corner of the table.

—At this phenomenon unheard-of in chess, two pieces taking each other out, Chlammy had no words, while Sora answered mockingly.

"Heh-heh-heh, you fool. This version of chess is a simulation of real war, yes? I've never lost at *Civ* or *Daisenryaku*—did you think that you could defeat me at this game, which is just an outdated version of the same?"

Correct—it wasn't chess. It was a *strategy game*. Magic to maintain morale—well, well, quite a useful spell. But something like that was only on the level of a status modifier like a *Social Policy* or *World Wonder*. And—he already knew well the weakness of such modifiers. Namely, *that her play style would come to depend on them—*. And if he could see her play style—he couldn't lose.

"Third Pawn Company! Now is your chance—take the enemy bishop!"

Sora shouting orders with conviction, just going for the mate, his pieces moving loyally. But before the bishop—

—*The pawn turned black.*

""""——Wha?!"""""

The crowd raised their voices in astonishment. It was already a familiar sight. But now, for the first time—*Sora was part of it*. Sora's countenance revealed to Chlammy that this turn of events was clearly *unexpected*. She smirked...thinly and darkly, and spoke:

"'Brainwashing'—what an interesting expression you use. Brainwashing is certainly an option, in regards such as this."

Another piece that tried to attack was forcibly turned black.

Forced brainwashing—that meant that all attacks from his side would be sealed off.

…*Crap.*

——Crap. Crap crap crap crap crap crap crap crap crap!

Sora managed not to show it on his expression, but he realized he'd made a fatal error. Her cheat being *maintaining insane morale*—was what he'd *assumed*!

—It was just the mistake he had haughtily criticized Steph for a few days back, and now he'd *done it himself*! He'd failed—he'd failed he'd failed he'd failed he'd failed he'd failed! It was an obvious, epic fail! Once his enemy was cornered, bereft of room to care about appearances… Once she was losing for the loss, she might be prepared to expose her use of magic—once she was already losing, *she might try the cheats that originally shouldered her with a risk of getting caught! (Why didn't I think of it—I'm such a dolt!)*

"—All troops, retreat! The enemy is using brainwashing magic; stay away!"

Under Sora's overpowering direction, even the pieces that weren't supposed to be able to retreat started retreating with all the others, but.

"Heh-heh, you think you're a battlefield king? This king is quite a poseur, trying to bring up the rear himself!"

Under the command of Chlammy, crowing at the sight of victory, the enemy descended upon the king—i.e., *Sora*. Specifically, the enemy queen.

"Take that king's head, Queen! It's checkmate!"

"…Brother!"

As the hall filled with noise, even Shiro felt a threat and raised her voice. But—Sora pronounced to the oncoming piece.

"—O Queen, I entreat you to lay down your sword…for you are—beautiful."

……

"""——What?"""

The crowd, Chlammy, even Shiro gaped. As Sora spoke heated, passionate nothings to the piece—the queen.

"O Queen. Do you serve that king of your own accord, or are you trapped by circumstances—in any case, I would that you might ask your heart. Is yon king truly a king worthy of your service?"

Like a first-rate stage actor. With the sweet voice of the playboy of the century, Sora put together an elegant line of words. Truly as if he were a young, handsome monarch on the battlefield.

"That king who brainwashes his soldiers, his people, to use them as his swords, his tools—to say nothing of putting you in front to bear the arrows as he cowers at the back: Does he merit your beauty, or your sword? O Queen, whose beauty I have but glimpsed on this field where strange fate has pit us against each other, I beseech you to lay down your sword and see—your people, those you should protect—your king! Where are they!"

—*Clank*—. With the sound of a sword falling to the ground.

—This time, *the black queen turned white.*

The crowd, still left agape, could no longer even make a sound. All that was left was Chlammy, who was speechless, and Sora, who just chuckled.

"——Wha——!"

"Heh-heh-heh, *romance simulation games* are one of the few genres I'm better than my sister at."

"——You little…!"

As Chlammy gnashed her teeth, the crowd sighed as if relieved. Seeing that Sora had done the same thing as the enemy, evening the match once more—that was probably why.

—*But that was wrong. So very wrong.* This—Sora was only able to do because he was the king and the enemy was the queen. But Chlammy—it was hard to say exactly, but it looked as if she could use any piece to brainwash another. While this side was still sealed off from attacking, the enemy carried on attacking freely. What lay ahead was nothing less than *certain defeat.*

—*What to do. What to do what to do* Sora—*virgin, eighteen*—! Sora put everything he had into holding up the unconcerned smirk floating on his face. With all his soul and fire, he looked for a way to somehow break the impasse. No—more accurately, he'd found a way. *There is—a way. Strictly speaking, there is… But will she fall for it?!*

—It would be a wild gamble. If it were successful, he'd *get by* for now. But, if he blew it—his last chance at victory would be gone. Compared to the risk of placing the bet, *the reward would be all too transient*—should he still lay it on the table? As Sora spun around his thoughts, in time compressed by excess secretion of neurotransmitters.

Now, this time, Shiro. Softly enclosed her brother's face…in her two small hands.

"——Wha…?"

The sudden sensation of warmth on his cheeks made his body want to leap. But Shiro peered into Sora's eyes and continued quietly.

"…You said…if you lost your cool, I should help you."

"——!"

"…Together…we are Blank…"

Yeah…

"—Yeah, we are…"

"……It's okay."

—You think she'll fall for it? To the silent question of the brother's eyes, the sister slightly, yet strongly…nodded. Once.

—That's right, Shiro—this genius girl—the sister he was so proud of, *had at a point outplayed an opponent unbound by rules that yet constricted her.* Only by reading her opponent's—Chlammy's—moves could she do such a thing. She may have been greatly the inferior of her brother in mind games and diplomacy—but Sora reminded himself.

—Don't forget. His sister *had defeated a god.*

That sister, by pure reading of moves, had stated unequivocally that she'd fall for it. Then all he had to do was trust his sister and form a strategy on that premise!

And so—Chlammy, shoulders shaking.

"Knight! Slay the traitor queen!"

——She fell for it…… She stepped right in—to the trap. The black knight commanded trembled as if conflicted, and then—. *Turned white.*

"H—how…Wh-*what did you do*?!"

—This was it. This was the one way out. If Chlammy really did mean to fight for the human race, it was the one thing she couldn't take: *It was her reaction to betrayal.* And the fact that she *still assumed that our heroes were cheating…* Here it was: the only scenario that could lead to victory. *Oh, that's my sister.* He told her by stroking her head, and she closed her eyes in pleasure like a cat.

And so, as if all things were preordained, Sora let out an impudent grin and spoke.

"King, foolish king. To order your subjects to kill their queen… Cruel commands are not well given. Perhaps you should cool your head. Those shoulders, shaking in anger—they are not fit to show your people."

"You—*damned traitor…!*"

Chlammy believed Sora to be cheating using the technology of another country—to be selling out his own people. Her face no longer bore that corpselike sense of helplessness, or of responsibility, but only rage. In contrast, Sora's face was bold, brazen, and full of ease.

…Who could have guessed it? That at that very moment, Sora himself felt his heart pounding hard enough to rupture, his mind in total mobilization. In his brain, he dug up all the knowledge he had yet acquired, through quiz games, through history games. All the wars he could possibly be expected to know of, and he simulated them.

—Indeed, *the situation had not improved a bit.* This wasn't a trick he could pull off indefinitely. It was only a bluff to buy time as the enemy fell into paranoia. If he were to charge defiantly onto the offensive, everything would be balanced on a tightrope demanding too-precise calculation. In that case—he could only find a way to win without fighting———

Win without fighting?

———.

—And, thus. In the midst of a situation tantamount to *certain defeat.* In the back of Sora's mind, a ray of light was finally found.

"—Shiro. Take command of the troops. Can you run them around so they won't be brainwashed by the enemy?"

"…That's easy."

His sister gave a firm salute, not needing to hear the reason, and took command.

—This, *again*, was a wild gamble. However, this time, *if successful, it meant certain victory*. To draw victory from the situation—there were only two ways. Ways in which Sora knew one could win without fighting—and they were.

"O Queen—"

Leaving his sister to lash out the orders, Sora spoke to the former enemy queen, now on his side.

"I dream not to ask you—nor those proud knights who lay down their swords out of love for you—to turn your blades on your brethren. This battle, this situation…already, anyone's eyes can see it for a vain butchery—while your king—already boils in the depths of madness."

Then Sora, in about the time a clock's second hand takes to move once. Turned through tens of thousands of words in his brain, and embarked on the seduction of a lifetime.

"Your people belong to you—already, I believe there is none but you to lead your people in the place of the *frenzied, mad king*—is this not the truth?"

As for Sora's speech and its intent—no one in the castle, not even Chlammy, could comprehend it. And so the castle hushed, as had happened many times so far. *Something beyond imagination was about to happen*—that they waited for in silence. And—finally, was it a result that answered their expectations?

The queen which had been black—which now was white.

—*This time, turned red.*

And, in continuity, *almost every black piece on the front line turned red.*

"——Huhh?!"

The cry came from Chlammy alone. The rest of the crowd must not have been able to grasp what had happened. However, Sora's speech continued—and finally made it clear.

"I celebrate your independence, O brave, admirable queen! You champions of justice, who have overcome brainwashing to follow your queen! I ask you not to slay your brethren! But they themselves surely wish not to slay you! It is you who must put an end to the oppression of this mad king, who brainwashes his people and robs them of their freedom!"

Indeed, it was. *The spark of insurrection—the emergence of a third force.*

"What I seek is not blood! It is what everyone seeks—yea, I seek *peace*! I would that our sides sheathe their swords; I shall not permit this bloodshed to go on!"

At this speech, the side of the red queen was joined by more and more red pieces.

—They might not hesitate to harm their enemies. But.

"—Y-you... No matter! Execute all renegades!"

Chlammy, raging without grasping the meaning, once more—walked into a trap.

"Another mistake, fool king. It is a universal truth, since time immemorial, that *armed suppression* of insurrection—is the worst move."

—Even if they would harm their enemies, the comrades with whom they had fought—regardless of brainwashing magic—would not be so easy to slay. Indeed, just as Sora had spoken, the pieces ordered by Chlammy turned red, one after another.

"—Wha... You... What is this; what is your trick!"

Chlammy had gone so far as to call on the power of elves to protect the human race. Her emotions regarding her own betrayal strengthened and stole away her composure. Meanwhile.

"...All troops, aid the red queen forces... Form a circle... Let...no one die."

Shiro took Sora's cue and issued appropriate directions to incorporate the red pieces into their battle strategy. But not really. Really she was just making it hard for Chlammy's army to attack *by using the red queen forces as a shield*. But she papered over that with words, *and manipulated the red queen's pieces to create a situation in which no one could get an attack through.*

—The result.

"——!—You treasonous swine!"

Chlammy ground her teeth and spewed bile. Yes—the result was that that *the battle deadlocked.*

"—Hey, mad king, I mean, 'brainwashing king,' have you heard?"

Sora explained with a smile as if this was what he had been aiming for all along.

"In real wars—you don't necessarily have to capture the king to win, you know? Come on, you already have no chance to win. Neither of us can do anything in this state—it's time for you to *resign.*"

Sparking an insurrection to split the nation's forces and forcing a *truce* from the overwhelmingly superior position this afforded: This was one of the ways Shiro knew to *win without fighting.* It probably appeared to the crowd that all of this was planned from the beginning. At the brilliant turnabout, the castle heated up, and a feverish roar resounded.

—Excluding one person. Yes—Chlammy alone glared daggers at Sora. She snickered.

"Heh-heh…heh-heh-heh… Don't underestimate me—I'll never hand over this country!"

It was a cackle like that of a true mad king. As the furor of the castle hushed, Chlammy gave her orders.

"All troops, lay down your lives and take the enemy king's head… All you have to do is follow my orders——*just cut down all traitors in your path.*"

It couldn't be detected by Sora—by Immanity. But the brainwashing magic must have grown even stronger. Unsettlingly, quietly, the black army began to advance. As did the red pieces, and the white pieces. The lines of pieces emanating the clear feeling that they were going to wipe out everything without regard, the castle swallowed.

"…Brother, this is what happens…when you back a weakened enemy into a corner."

As even his sister pointed it out with a trace of cold sweat. Even so, Sora smiled back.

"I know—that's why I did it."

Crik—

The sound came out of nowhere. The black king, Chlammy's king.

—Developed a crack.

"—Uh—wha-what?"

As the crack spread through the black king. And Chlammy watched in shock, not knowing what was going on, Sora told her plainly.

"Dictators of continual oppression, subjugation by fear, and brainwashing—it's a funny thing."

This was—*the second way* Shiro knew to *win without fighting*.

"It works when you're winning, but once you start losing, universally, for some reason, such leaders' fates are always sealed in the same way."

…Namely.

"It has held true for time immemorial: *Their fate is sealed by assassination by someone close to them, who's not even a combat unit.*"

—A historical fact of the world they came from, repeated endlessly. The brainwashing expanded in scope; appearances were abandoned. Becoming vilified as a *despot*, being run to the edge of defeat. Commanding as a *mad king*, and thus—*self-destructing*.

And so, watching the cracked-apart black king crumble. Everyone in the castle. Even Chlammy stood stunned.

"Sorry, *our world* isn't as nice a place as this one."

Victorious, rising from the seat, Sora and Shiro.

"—When it comes to conflict and slaughter, compared to you, we're seasoned experts."

And then he heaved a single great sigh. Sora exchanged a quick high five with Shiro, and his eyes grew distant. Their *old* world. Squinting as if to look at it far, far off.

"But here, it ends with a game. This is a fine world…"

…So he murmured.

■■■

"W-wow…"

—The scene of victory was overwhelming, dazzling. Amidst the cheers that shook the entire castle, it was Steph who whispered. The cheering spectators probably didn't understand the underlying truth. Steph alone did. Not to say she understood all of the siblings' tactics and statements. Since she had no way of knowing what *their world* was like. But. She knew that that girl—Chlammy—had received powerful Elven backup. That the game that had just unfolded hid their cheating magic. And, in the end, that *they had faced that magic head-on and broken through*. This meant—albeit indirectly—that they had faced the world's largest country, Elven Gard, and defeated them. That *mere humans had triumphed* over a magic-using race. An accomplishment with not a single precedent in the history that Steph knew of. And, therefore—

"......Are they really human?"

In awe—even fear, she couldn't help but whisper this. In contrast to the uproar of the audience, the vanquished Chlammy looked down in silence. As the siblings slid away from the table without a second glance at her. And as they walked up to Steph, Steph, for a moment—didn't know what to do.

—Because they'd brought down face-on an enemy that cheated with magic, and they weren't even showing triumph.

—" " *doesn't lose...*—

When the two stood there as if to prove this, without surprise at their victory, what was she supposed to say? But—with no inkling of the conflict within Steph, Sora spoke playfully.

"—Does this do it for you?"

"......Uh?"

"Now no one's gonna call your grandfather—*the old king—a fool*, right?"

"——Oh..."

"If, without anyone's backing, *we, the strongest of the humans, became the monarch*—that means he was wise."

"...Now, Elkia...won't die; aren't... you glad...Steph?"

Searching for words, at a loss. She did think back to all the things they'd done to her. But the result more than made up for it all. Dew droplets welled up in her eyes as she decided to admit it out loud.

"Thank you...I'm so—grateful to you...ooh—"

Choking up a bit, Steph wondered if she was clearly understandable. But Shiro stretched up and patted her on the head. It was not possible any longer for Stephanie Dola to hold back the tears.

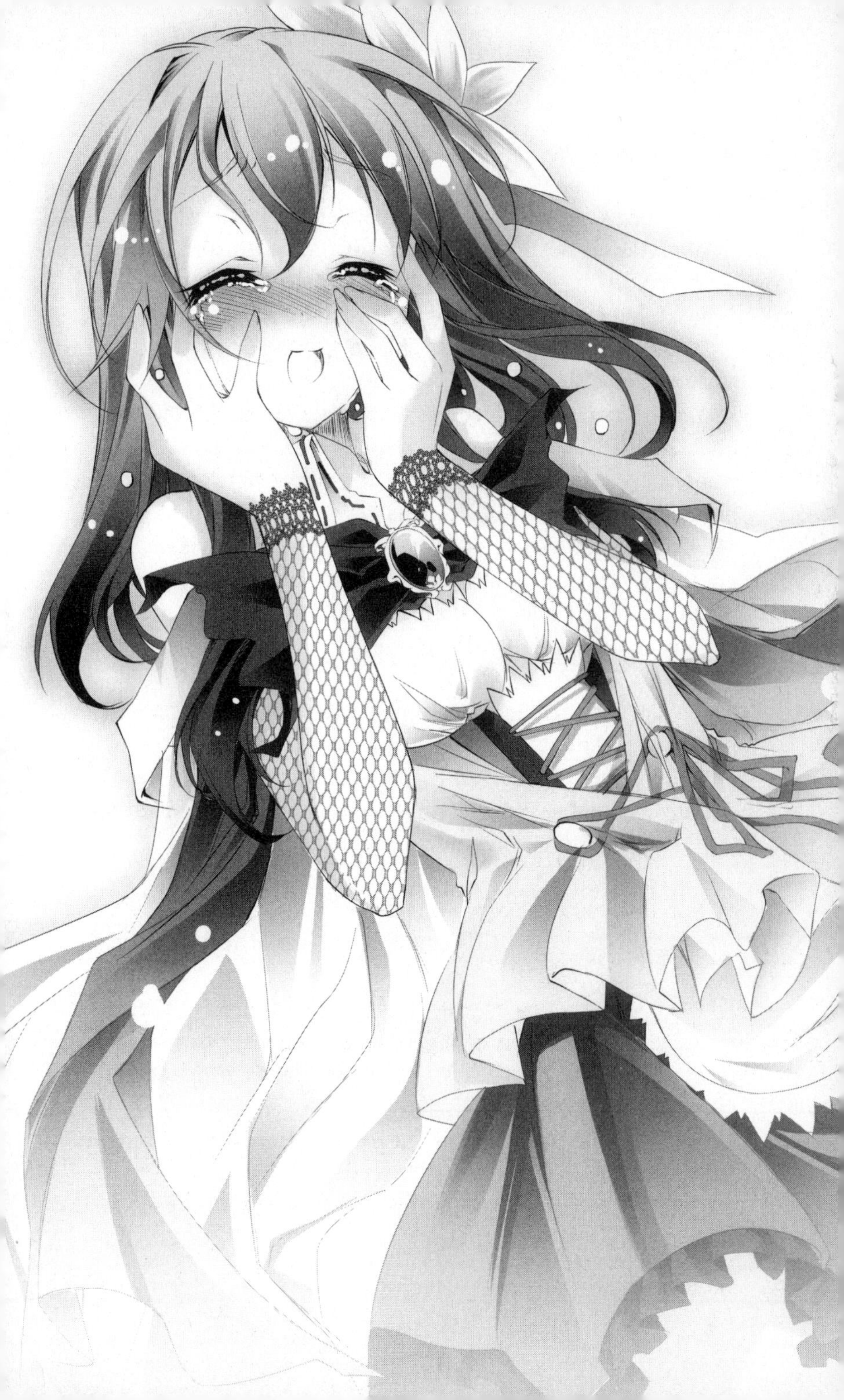

—And with that.

"......Hey."

Chlammy's mumble fell out and was erased by the cheers roaring through the castle. But, in the ears of Sora, Shiro, and Steph alone, it rang cold.

"Just tell me... What manner of trick did you use?"

With these cold, low words, Chlammy pierced Sora with a scowl, and continued.

"Yes, it's true. I accepted the help of the Elves. As the only way for humans to survive. And now you've ruined it. Now answer me, whose spies are you? Certainly you don't mean to tell me that a mere human was able to defeat elven magic!"

From her perspective, he was a loathsome enemy who had sold out Immanity. As Chlammy interrogated Sora with eyes full of hate, Steph swallowed—but the siblings.

"I do, and, *actually, I did.*"

"...You got a problem?"

The cheers roaring through the castle subsided as Sora walked back toward Chlammy.

"You know, I did mean it when I said that your plan wasn't bad, and if you could prove your story was true about getting Elven help for the sake of Immanity, I could have even stepped down."

"Then why—!"

"But I don't like the way you think."

Sora looked down at Chlammy with a scornful gaze that was no act.

"If it's 'We're gonna use the Elves and claw our way up,' that's one thing, but when you're saying, 'We can't even survive without the protection of the great Elves,' that seemed just a little too pathetic, and it kinda pissed me off."

"—Hasn't that been proven? The limits of Immanity, by history, by the present we're in!"

While Chlammy looked at him as if to imply, How can you talk when I know you cheated, too?

"Those are the limits of those dudes who made history; they sure ain't *our limits…*"

With these nasty words, he smiled.

"Humans have their own way of doing things. Like, yeah—the way we won because *you always believed that we were cheating to the end.*"

Now swallowing, looking back at the match, Chlammy. She'd been totally wrapped up in uncovering the ruse they were using, but what if. What if *there had never been any ruse in the first place—*?

"That…can't be… A mere human—couldn't possibly…compete with magic."

"If that's what you think, that's fine; that's your limit."

And Sora squinted.

"Whether the opponent be elven *or a god*, the word 'lose' isn't in Blank's dictionary."

With that—as if to signify that her pride had been sullied—Sora took hold of Chlammy's chin and peeled off the black veil. Then looking straight into her eyes, Sora for the first time showed faint anger lurking in his own—and he spoke.

"Don't—*underestimate humans like that.*"

……Those words hushed everyone in the castle. They echoed and spread, as if soaking into their hearts. As if to rend the chains that bound them as inadequate humans. As if piercing an epoch of darkness with a single ray of light.

—As if lighting the lamp of a quiet hope in their hearts.

—Then, a word fell from Chlammy's mouth as well.

"Wuh——"

"…Wuh?"

"WAAAAAAAAAAAAAAAAAAAAAAAAAAAAAAAAAAAAAAA AAAAAAAAAAAAAAAAAAAAAẠAAAAAAAAAAAAAAAAAAAA AAAAAAAAAAAAAAAAAAAAAH!"

"Whoa! What the hell?!"

Suddenly, Chlammy dropped to the floor and started wailing. Sora, not knowing what to do, took a step back in surprise—and who could blame him.

"Waaaah, you're so stupid; I hate you! Don't you know...how hard, *hic*, it—it was to make contracts so I could get the Elves and then trash them... I-I-I-I-I wasn't underestimating anything; I was serious! Waaah..."

As Chlammy spilled out big tears, opened her mouth wide, and bawled, everyone was astonished. Whether it was the reaction from the load on her being removed, or whether that was her *real personality*—in any case, it seemed it was universally agreed in every world that there's nothing you can do about crying children.

"...Brother...made a girl...cry..."

"Hey, wait, it's my fault?!"

"Waaaaahhhhhhhhhhhh...stupid...jerk...just diiie..."

The crowd, who until just recently had been roaring in victory, now just looked vaguely on at Chlammy as she hurled insults between childish sobs——

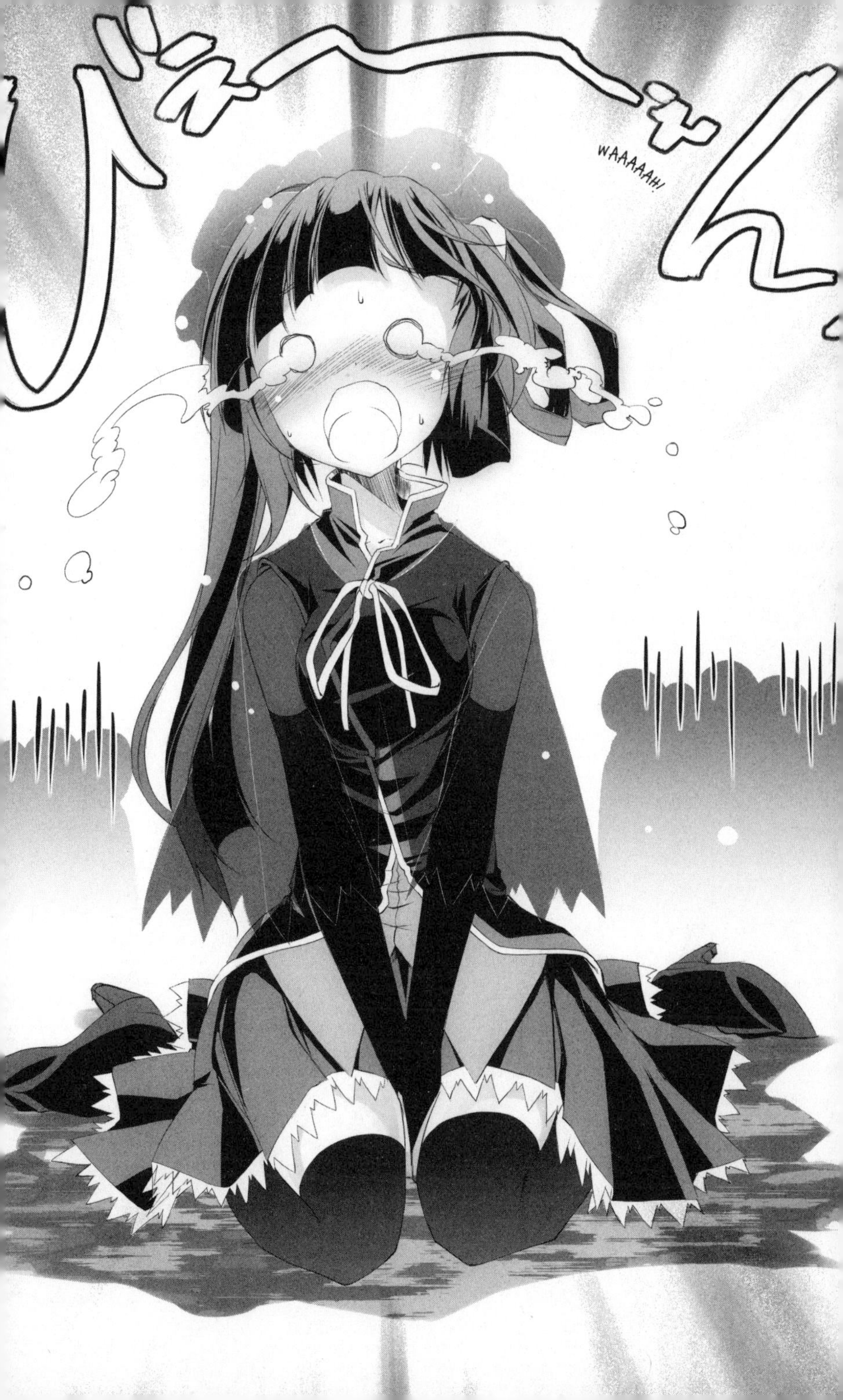
WAAAAAH!

⏻ CHAPTER 4
GRANDMASTER

Chlammy wailed: Stupid jerk, I hate you, I'll never give in, I'll show everyone about you—etc., to the end, and finally left as if running away.

"Good grief… What's the point if even humans themselves start underestimating humans…?"

At Sora's words of vexation, the castle once again was enveloped in acclamation.

—A victory too complete to question. A victory that showed everyone unmistakably the promise of the humans' new monarch. Cheers thundered throughout the Great Hall and carried forward the steps of the elderly official with crown in hand.

"Well, then—your name is Sora, correct?"

"Yeah."

"Will you accept the crown of the Kingdom of Elkia?"

But Sora announced back decisively.

"*No.*"

And, bringing his sister close, he said with a smile:

"Together, we are Blank—we two are the monarch."

This had been mentioned during the chess match as well. The crowd raised their voices higher—celebrating the birth of a new king and a little queen.

—But.

"—Unfortunately, that is not possible."

"—Huh?"

The cheers halted at the official's words.

"Wha? Uh, why not?"

"The Ten Covenants stipulate that *'an agent plenipotentiary'* be established. There cannot be two."

The buzzing hall, the siblings looking at each other. Sora pondered fretfully, scratched his head, furrowed his brow…and spoke.

"…I see. Uh, so, we'll split roles and have me take this on, yeah?"

"……Ng."

Setting down his sister, who groaned minutely, Sora turned back to face the official.

"Then we'll resume—*ahem*. I hereby crown Sora the 205th monarch of the Kingdom of Elkia—if any among you object, speak now! If not, your silence shall—"

—But someone who could not hold her peace interrupted, raising her hand.

"…Mm."

Long white hair. A girl through whose bangs peeped ruby-red eyes—but seriously.

"Uh, Shiro?"

"…I have an objection."

"Umm, pardon, my sister? Whatever do you speak of?"

"…If you become king…you can build a harem."

"————————What?"

Though Sora answered as if he didn't believe his ears, still Shiro scrunched her face as if about to cry and spoke.

"…And then you won't……need…me."

Paying no attention to the bewildered audience, flustered to an improbable degree, Sora spoke.

"Hey! Heyheyhey, wait wait that's ridiculous! You and I, together we're one team, right! It's just for formality's sake; I'll be the king technically, but it's not like—"

"...But you'll be—the king... I'll be just there. It can be only one...so—"

After she smudged off her tears with her arm, there were no more tears.

"...It'll be—me."

In the sister's unemotional eyes dwelled a clear will to fight. As they pierced her brother with a declaration of war—

"——Huh?"

Sora, on the other end of that stare, changed his own expression.

"Hey now... My darling, precious sister. It's rare to hear you tell jokes; how's the weather in hell?"

Grinning with his usual frivolous attitude. But with a clear hostility in his tone of voice.

"See what happens if a thousand-ships-level beauty like you becomes queen. You're too innocent. You might get taken in by some sweet-talking bum—your brother can't let you be queen."

Though Sora faced Shiro spewing the ultimate doting-brother lines. Contrary to his words that suggested almost-smothering love, there was no hint of a smile in his eyes.

"...No, Brother, you can't be king—that's final."

"—Bring it on, then. 'Cause your brother's not gonna let *you* be king. And that's final."

Two gazes, facing each other, clashing. The gazes of the two who had overcome even Elven cheating to attain the human race's most powerful title. They weren't the gazes of the intimate siblings, nor those of the two-in-one gamer " ". They were the gazes of *long rivals*, and their wills looked firm enough to draw sparks...

"Eh, well... In that case, shall I take it that you two wish to settle this with a final match?"

It must have required considerable courage to come between them. To the official, checking with them apologetically.

"Sure, I'm ready."

"...That's fine."

Without hesitation. And without looking away, they laid down the gauntlet.

"I'm not gonna go easy on you, my sister. Today's the day you're goin' down."

"…Worry about yourself…Brother… Today, I'm serious."

——……

—And so. *Three days* passed.

In the center of the hall, among the scattered remains of countless games played back-to-back without sleep or rest. The siblings lay sprawled on the floor.

"…Hey…why don't…you give up already?"

"…Why don't you…just resign."

The countless games that had begun under the condition of *two consecutive wins for victory*. Totaled—five hundred: 158 wins, 158 losses, 184 draws.

—The tragedy was that, never mind in this place, even back in their old world. While " " had risen to the status of an urban legend—no one knew *the match records between the two*. Aside from their collective name as " ". The two game-loving siblings, as a matter of the most natural course, played each other. And their records were—

—3,526,744 games, 1,170,080 wins, 1,170,080 losses, 1,186,584 draws——

…To this day, neither had ever *gotten ahead or behind once*. The people in the castle had no way of knowing this tragic fact as they waited for the coronation. But by now they'd long since gone home.

—Then come back, then all gone home again. As they tried to predict when would be a good time, gradually, fewer and fewer people came at all. The castle staff lay sprawled across the Great Hall—even the presiding official, with crown in hand, and Steph, who each were just barely holding on to consciousness, were already well into the land of hallucinations. Every now and then, the old official would grin creepily and then return to a normal expression. Meanwhile, Steph reached out at air with a blank smile, saying, "Oh, a butterfly."

—So, what should the next game be… As Sora thought about it in his hazy head. A question popped up and stayed his hand.

"Hey… Why does the monarch have to be one person?"

"…What?"

To these words, the official and Steph responded, brought back from la-la land. To articulate his concern, Sora took out his phone. And read out his notes on the Ten Covenants once more.

"The Seventh of the Ten Covenants: *'For conflicts between groups, an agent plenipotentiary shall be established'…*"

This was a rule that directed groups—i.e., countries and races—each to designate a representative for conflicts between them.

—But. Sora, having pronounced it carefully, meditatively, made sure there was no contradiction between the words he'd reread and pronounced and the conclusion he'd reached. "—Does it actually say anywhere it has to be an individual?" he murmured.

"""_____"""

—And, thus the legendary struggle, of which the bards would later sing of as the "Nightmare Three Days," came to a close. But, it being an inordinately long story, let us pass over it in this account…

■■■

……——.

"…Hey, is this really okay?"

"Sure it is. Since times of yore, monarchs who have clad themselves in ostentatious garb have generally done so to hide their baseness within, to inflate their public image and aggrandize themselves. A monarch should be a model for the people, an ideal to emulate—reverence should be won by deeds."

"…So…full of it…"

"Yeah, okay, to be honest, I just feel the most comfortable like this."

"*Hh*… Fine, as you wish. But at least do something about your hair."

The capital city, Elkia—the grand square in front of the castle. Coming out onto the castle veranda, the sweeping plaza reminds one of Piazza San Marco in Venice. Now the square was filled with a throng of countless people. How many thousands—how many tens of thousands of people were there? Yearning to hear the words of their new king, the crowd spilled out of the square into the streets extending from it. It was an expression of their loss of hope in the previous king, scorned as a fool. An expression of their need for a thread of hope for Immanity, left standing in a pit of despair. An expression that they sought from the siblings, who had taken down an Elven spy—taken down magic—head-on. On the castle veranda, where gathered the gazes, pregnant with expectation, of the entire human race—two figures stepped out. A young man and a girl. A young man with dark circles under his eyes, wearing jeans and a T-shirt that read "I ♥ PPL." A girl with long hair white enough to make one think of snow and white skin to match, along with eyes red as jewels and a sailor suit. Their crowns told that they were the king and the queen.

—But. The young man had contorted the queen's tiara and looped it onto his arm like an armband. Meanwhile, the girl had tied up her hair with the king's crown, lifting her bangs—. Seeing them, it was easy to imagine why Steph had cried out during their changing.

In this half-assed getup, standing before his dazed people, the young man—Sora—spoke up.

"Uhh…mm, mmng. Umm, good day."

"…Brother, you're nervous. Unusual."

"—Shut up. You know we're both afraid of crowds. Normally I'm just repressing it."

Shiro gently took her brother's hand, careful not to let the crowd see her do it.

"……"

Silently. As if to say, Then repress it again now. As if to say, Just as you always have—and you always will.

"—My esteemed people—no, comrades of Immanity!"

As if he had grasped his sister's intent, the brother raised his voice with a face from which the tension had dissolved. A bullhorn was attached to the veranda railing, but he bellowed with a fierce power that suggested he didn't need it.

"We, Immanity…under the Ten Covenants, in this world without war, have lost continually until we have been reduced to our last country, our last city—*why is this*?"

The crowd was taken aback at the sudden question thrown at them.—Because of the old king's mistakes.—Because we can't use magic. Sora waited for each to come up with an answer and then continued.

"Because the old king failed? Because we are the lowest-ranking race? Because we cannot use magic? Because our race is destined to die helplessly?!—Nay!"

The strong denial made the air and the masses alike tremble. Making a fist and no effort to hide his emotions, Sora shouted on.

"In the past, in the Great War of the ancient gods, the gods, the devils—the Elves, the Werebeasts, so many races struggled against each other, and we fought, and we survived! In the past, the entirety of this continent was the domain of human countries—then *why is this*!"

On the basis of the history he had read through in the past few days in Steph's library, Sora asked them.

"Is it because we are a race skilled in violence? Is it because we are a race specializing in combat?!"

Everyone in the audience looked at each other.

"We have not the diverse magic of the Elf, nor the physical prowess of the Werebeast, nor the longevity of the Flügel—this being so, did our former dominion over this continent result from specialization in combat?—By no means!!"

Yes, this was a clear fact that anyone could see. But then came a question.

—Then why?

"We survived through combat because we were *weak*!

"In all ages, in all worlds, *the strong hone their fangs and the weak their wisdom*! Why have we been backed into a corner—it is only because the Ten Covenants have torn out the fangs of the strong and forced them to hone *their* wisdom!

"What we believed to be our exclusive property as the *weak*—ingenuity, strategy, tactics, the power to survive!—was obtained by the strong as well! Our wisdom was seized by the strong, and we faced the strong with the same weapons—that is what has brought us to these depths!"

With the desperate situation laid out, the square fell silent. The gathered audience was enveloped in such emotions as dejection, despair, and discomfort. Sora looked around at them with a sigh and went on.

"All you here, answer me, why do you hang your heads?"

Sora, once raging and swinging his fist, now spoke softly.

"Let me repeat: We are the *weak*. Indeed, *still we are—just as we always have been—*"

Someone took in a sudden breath, realizing something. After waiting for it to spread, Sora shouted out once more.

"—Indeed…is not the situation *exactly the same*?

"The strong may imitate the wisdom of the weak, but they will never attain true mastery! For the truth underlying our weapon—is the *cowardice* born of abject weakness!"

The crowd's question was preemptively answered.

"Who, through cowardice, has honed their eyes and ears, their wit, to *learn* to survive? It is we humans!"

They were shown hope in despair.

"We cannot use magic. We cannot even perceive it—however, cowardice has given us *the wit to escape magic, the wisdom to see through it*! We have no supernatural senses. However, cowardice has given us, through learning and experience, *wisdom approaching precognition*!"

…One who speaks only of hope is an optimist.

…And one who speaks only of despair is a pessimist.

"For the third time! We are the *weak* who, throughout the ages, *have torn out the throats of the complacent strong—we are the proud weak!*"

…The deeper the despair and darkness, the more it was true.

"I announce that my sister and I have been crowned here as your king and queen, as the 205th monarch of Elkia."

...That only one who lights the watch fire of hope can attract the masses.

"I announce that the two of us shall live as the weak, fight as the weak, and *slaughter the strong as the weak do*! *Just as we always have—and just as we always will!*"

...So people look to their steps as a guide.

"Accept it! We are the weakest race!

"We are those who, in endless cycles of history—devour the fattened strong!"

...Thus.

"Take pride! For we are the weakest—we are *the most empty-handed*! We are born with nothing—*and so we can become anything*—and we therefore are the strongest race!"

...A monarch is born.

Cheers—no, *roars* followed. They shook the square, the sky. The shouts that could sound like howls of rage, or cries of victory. Out of expectation for the two on the platform? Or—out of the souls of the cornered, baring their fangs?

Before this sight, Sora and his sister looked at each other.

......The sister nodded. Slightly, with a pleasant smile. With this confirmation, Sora started his final speech. Spreading his arms wide, innocent as a giddy child. Yet like a strategist who'd seen it all, bold as a warrior. Spreading across his face a guileless yet brazen smile, Sora—the new king of the human race—spoke.

"—Come, let the games begin!

"Surely you have had your fill of suffering. Surely you have been humiliated too much. Surely you have tasted life's bitterness to the point of sickness... Surely this is enough! Here I am, my fellow Immanities."

His palm rose to the horizon, as if he might even clutch the heavens. And then—closed.

"Now, as of this moment! We, Elkia—*declare war on all other countries in the world*!

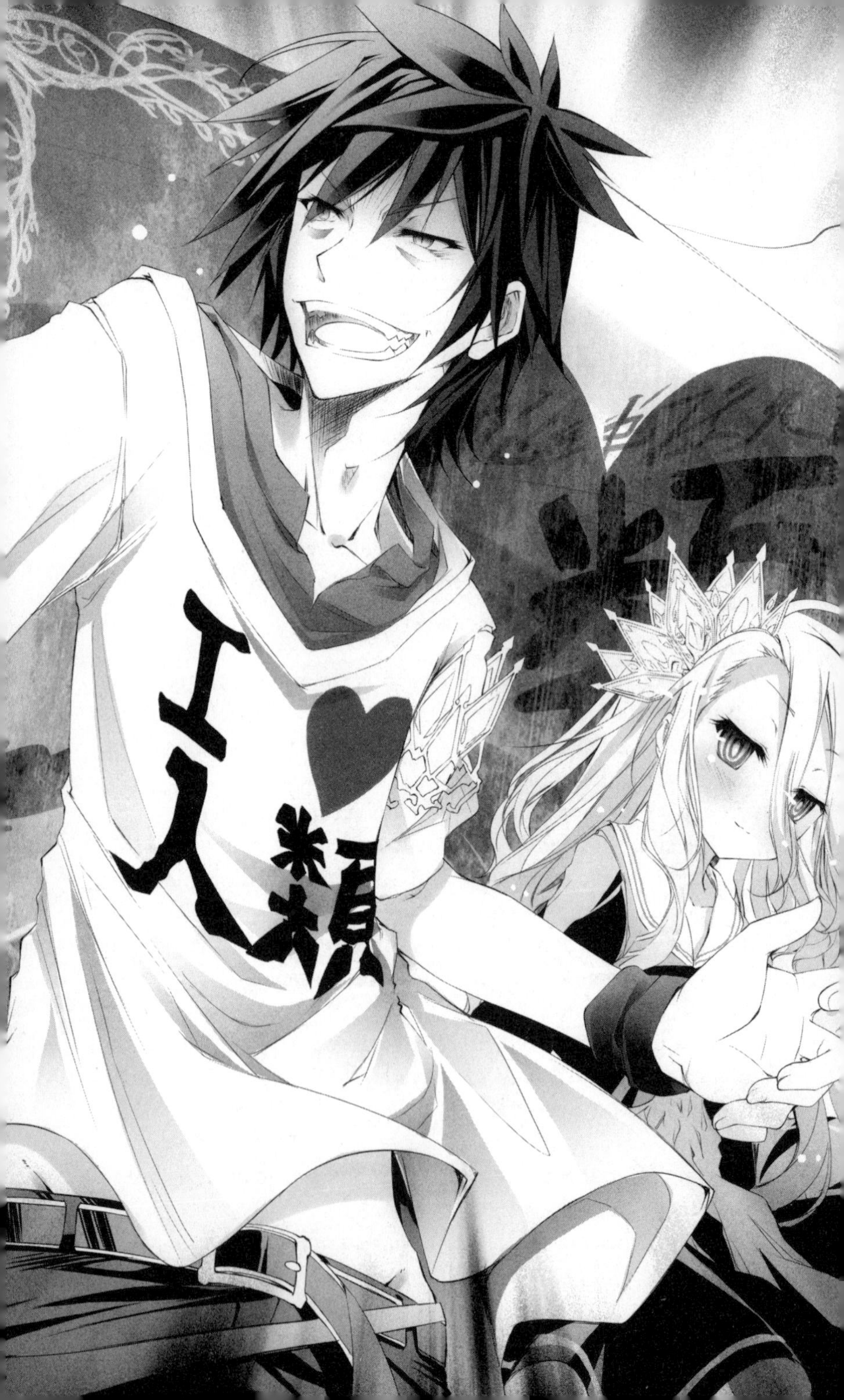
I ♥ 人類

"Light the signal for a counterstrike! We will have our borders back!"

■■■

Amidst cheers so great as to split the earth. The two left the stage, to be attacked by Steph.

"H-h—hey, you! Wh-what the heck are you talking about?!"

"Aaagh...what're you freaking out about, Steph? You're freaking *me* out."

"...Steph, so creepy..."

With Steph honking and bleating in mad disorder, the siblings sneered at her unjustifiably. But Steph had bigger things on her mind.

"You think everything's okay now?! You just got crowned and haven't even taken care of domestic affairs yet, and you think Elkia is ready to take on other countries? Are you trying to destroy the nation?!"

Steph clutched her head and cursed her own foolishness for believing in these swindler siblings, though perhaps she was getting used to it. With a gesture that suggested he was already in his element, Sora spoke with a sigh.

"*Hhh...* Look—didn't I tell you to learn to doubt people?"

"—Huh?"

Steph stopped in her tracks and fixated on Sora.

"After the Elves—Elven Gard, right?—went as far as to get Chlammy working for them to try to take over this country, you think they're going to think *they were beaten face-on by mere humans who can't use magic*?"

"—Wh-what do you mean?"

"Did you forget? They think we're *people with the support of another country*. At the very least, whoever was supporting Chlammy must be reporting it that way, and it's probably what the other countries think, too."

The sister continued her brother's words as if to supplement them.

"…The world thinks…a spy from some other country has taken over Elkia."

Her brother nodded and went on.

"But they don't know which country. They don't know whose spy, whose puppet is running the country, and then suddenly we declare war on the whole world, and this is what they think—'Some country has installed a puppet government in Elkia and is ready to go on the offensive'—right?

"——Oh—"

In this world's contests, the challenged party had the right to determine the game. So it was in spite of the fact that *taking the offensive was extremely disadvantageous* that they had *declared war on the whole world*. And also considering that they had defeated the spy of Elven Gard—

"They're going to be worried that now there's some country, some race, that's got a trump card that can even beat the Elves, right?"

"…So."

"To throw the whole world into paranoia…"

"…*We're going and declaring war on them…*"

"…*And then not doing anything.* See?"

The siblings' smiling words left Steph speechless.

"The Fifth of the Ten Covenants: 'The party challenged shall have the right to determine the game.' When all those countries we declared war against get worried, they'll probably, like…try to figure out what country is backing us, even though there is none. While the whole world is stretching itself to try to pry into us, let's pry back *their* armor, find their weak spots, and solidify our base."

To the brother who smirked, spoke, and turned his back, Steph asked:

"S-so…when you said you were going to take back our land…you were…lying?"

Steph surprised herself with her significant feeling of regret. Perhaps it was due to a momentary aggressiveness stirred up by Sora's speech. Or perhaps—

"—Hey, Steph. I talked it over with my sister—whether we want to go back to our old world."

"——Uh?"

"There was nothing to talk about. Our answer is *No*—there would be no point whatsoever in abandoning a world as fun as this one to go back to that one."

"…Especially…for us."

"So, there you go. Now."

Clapping his hands together, Sora.

"We are humans. The last country of Immanity is this one, Elkia. To prevent it from disappearing, we have set our objective as taking the throne for now—but?"

The sister and the brother. Exchanging looks, laughing happily.

"Okay, my sister?"

"…Mm."

"The enemy can use magic. They can use superpowers. We can't. We're at an overwhelming disadvantage, playing against an overwhelming handicap; we have only one city left in our territory; the situation is hopeless. However, to protect the name of Blank, *we can't have a single loss*—what do you think?"

On the face of the sister, typically lacking in expression, a child-like smile emerged, and she answered in one word.

"…Sweet."

"I know, right?"

Steph, watching this exchange with eyes as if watching something unknown—something literally from another world. After lining up each of the conditions of a hopeless situation, the first word that came out was "sweet"—? To Steph, who had no idea what it was supposed to mean, Sora turned back.

"So, returning to your question, Steph."

"—Uh, *yes*?"

At being spoken to when she was out of it, her voice slipped into a falsetto.

"About taking back the borders. To be honest, that was a lie."

"——Uh?"

Sora, taking out his phone as he talked. Opening his task scheduler and putting a check by "being king." He input a new task. Namely—

"Final Objective—Conquer the world, for now!"

"—Wha—?!"

That Sora's words had gone past taking back the borders—past taking back the continent—to taking over the world. And at just how many times she could be surprised in one day, Steph made a sound with a double meaning. Sora twirled back and walked away with Shiro following him. Steph, finding herself being left alone, panicked and chased after them, discombobulated.

"Uh, um, umm, a-a-are you serious?!"

"Blank can't be anywhere but first place. Whether it's a play for dominion or whatever, if we're gonna play a *game*, our goal is to be the *only one at the top*—that's our rule."

Shiro nodded decisively.

—Now that it had come to this, all the more. Stephanie Dola had to realize that she'd still underestimated these siblings. Could it be? That against all odds it really was true? These two—

—could be the *saviors* of the human race?

She watched Sora's back as he departed, and her heartbeat quickened with a thump. Her chest tightened—but there was no more hatred in it. He'd restored her grandfather's honor. Saved her beloved country—saved Elkia. Declared he'd even take back its territory. Turned to go as if he actually could and would do it. His form, seen from behind—Stephanie Dola could no longer find a reason to hate it.

■■■

—In the Kingdom of Elkia, the capital, Elkia: Block 1, Central District…meaning the *Elkia Royal Castle: the royal bedchamber*. The king of Elkia, sprawled on a bed so huge one couldn't help but wonder just how many people were supposed to sleep there. A man who,

days before, had been a mere unemployed video game vegetable—
Sora (eighteen, virgin).

"—From a cramped gaming room to a dump inn room to Steph's
mansion and finally the royal bedchamber—huh."

Chuckling at a rise that would make a spaceman sick, Sora held a
book. The title of the book, lit in the darkness by the moon and dim
lighting: *The Ixseed Ecosystem*. Sora paused his eyes on the first page
and lost himself in thought.

"—Flügel…eh. These seem like guys I could get on my side…"

In the book it was explained: Flügel. A war race created as the
sky-soaring vanguard of gods in the ancient Great War. Since the
Ten Covenants, their combat abilities had been effectively sealed off.
Still, they possess enormous life spans and high magical aptitude,
which they had utilized in building a literal *city of the heavens* on the
back of Avant Heim (ä'-vänt häm'), a colossal Phantasma drifting
through the sky—which they preserve as their single territory without participating in play for dominion. However, perhaps because
of their long life spans, they do have a powerful *thirst for knowledge*,
and engage in games solely to obtain knowledge from the world's
other races—that is, to collect books.

"It sounds like they know a lot about magic, and I could draw
them in with my knowledge of another world."

If he could just make contact with this race somehow, it seemed it
would help in figuring out how to fight against magic—

—*Knock, knock.*

As he thought about such things, there was a reserved knock.
Feeling a déjà-vu-like sense that something like this had happened a
few days ago, he responded.

"Uh-huh, who is it?"

"It's—it is Stephanie Dola, Your Majesty… Can I—may I enter, Sir?"

"—Huh? Sure."

To Steph, who opened the heavy door of the royal bedchamber
with a deferent demeanor, Sora spoke.

"Hey, why are you talking and acting like that? Just come in like
normal."

"Well…you see, when I thought about it calmly—Sir—it is true that you are the king of Elkia, and thus—"

"Aaaah! That's so embarrassing!"

Sora interrupted Steph with a shout.

"That makes me feel all itchy and it takes too damn long! You can just talk like always; so, what?"

Electricity had not been discovered in Elkia. The royal bedchamber was illuminated only by the dim candle chandelier and the moon. In this faint light, Steph stood with her expression unreadable in the center of the room, unmoving.

"Then—Sora…"

"Right."

"You ordered me, 'Fall in love with me,' so that I would *fall at your feet*, correct?"

"Uh—yeaaahh…"

"Now that you have become the king of Elkia—I'm—now I'm…"

Through a gap in the clouds, for a moment, the moonlight strengthened, and Steph's expression became clear.

—It was anxious.

"Uh…so, you're saying, since I don't need you anymore anyway, you want me to release you from your covenant?"

"N-no! That's not what I mean!"

—There he was: for all his brilliance in games, an eighteen-year-old virgin. Flustered, Steph hastily corrected Sora's totally off-the-mark interpretation, then asked:

"I-I—want…to know. Wh-why you asked me, well, not to—be your possession, as your sister suggested, but to…fall in love with you."

"…Umm…"

It was due to ulterior motives. I.e., due to Sora's base desires, i.e., a *mistake*. As Sora contemplated whether he ought to admit this, a further unexpected question came first.

"So—did you make me fall in love with you…because, well, you had *that kind of feeling for me*?"

"……Huh?

"If—if that happens to be the case…I, uh—all I have left…"

With that, she walked up to the bed, and, with an uncomfortable yet beet-red face. She—*pulled up her skirt* and said in a pleading tone:

"…to give you now is…*this*, you know…"

—Hold on.

——Hold on, Sora, virgin, eighteen. You just got hit with an issue you can't overlook. I see…looking at Steph objectively…she is pretty hot. It's only natural that a healthy young man would want to be liked by a qt3.14 like her. But—*what did he want to do after making her fall in love with him?*

—*Love at first sight? Eh, I don't know about that.* He searched his heart, asking whether he really had romantic feelings for—

Wait—to begin with. (Huh—? Romantic feelings—*how are those even supposed to feel?*)

—Sora ran upon the inherent limitations of the dateless loser.

"…Well…that's, uh…"

Snap. A flash and a click. From the other side of the bed had emerged—Shiro, phone in hand.

"Ee—eeyaaaah!"

Seeing Shiro in the same room, Steph hastily lowered her skirt and retreated.

—But she should have realized it was a matter of course. Thinking back on the incident in the inn—*there was no way Sora could be by himself.*

"On behalf of…Brother…anguished by the limits…of the virgin—Shiro shall explain."

"Shiro… If I may be so bold, your brother finds it somewhat scarring to be told this by his eleven-year-old sister."

However, ignoring her brother's protest, Shiro showed the picture she had just taken. Showing *Steph with her skirt pulled up, showing her panties completely.*

"…This."

"—Hnh?"

"…is why Brother told you…to fall…in love with him."

Both Steph and Sora looked completely confused. Shiro explained bluntly so that even they would understand.

"…There is one thing…Brother misses…about our old world."

Which was that—

"…This, world—lacks…*porn*."

""———What?""

Questioning aloud were both Steph and Sora. But with different meanings. In Sora's case, it was a protest against an overly blunt demonstration. In Steph's case—

"'Pohrn'…? What do you mean?"

It was an innocent query. While manipulating her phone, Shiro responded.

"Materials…for fapping… Photographs, videos…etc.… Fantasies…to aid the fap. Collectively, they are called—*porn*…"

"Fap-ping?"

To Steph, who apparently still didn't understand, Shiro, still without expression.

Closed one hand loosely—*and pumped it up and down.*

"———Wha——"

As Steph's face reddened so violently it seemed it should make a boom, Shiro went further and started a video playing on her phone, then showed it to Steph.

—A video of Steph washing Shiro's hair: *the bath scene.*

"…Steph…this is…the meaning of your existence."

Steph's reddened face blanched, then dropped and quivered.

—So, anyone would do.

——All he wanted was an outlet for his sexual urges.

——And, on top of that, he was, *you know, doing that stuff while looking at his naked sister*?!

"Y-you're *scum!*"

Steph shouted and fled the room as Sora watched her, dazed. Then, to Shiro, who had returned to reading her book on the edge of the bed without apparent concern, he noted:

"—Hey, my thoughts aren't actually *that* dirty, y'know."

"…I summarized…"

"I think you mean *summit*-ized… And about that bath video? I thought you said it wasn't okay and *didn't ever let me see it*… Could it be you're trying to get Steph to hate me on purpose?"

"…I'm just eleven… I don't get this confusing stuff."

"You sure know how to act like a kid when it's convenient for you…"

"…You don't want the photo from just…now?"

"Oh, excuse me, Director. I am much obliged."

—However. After all—what was the difference between *romantic feelings* and *sexual desire*? As Sora pondered such philosophical questions of great weight to an eighteen-year-old virgin, in a voice too soft to hear, Shiro—his *sister who wasn't blood-related*—mumbled:

"…Just…seven more years…"

—They say girls mature emotionally faster than boys. Indeed…in this case, at least, that was an incontrovertible fact.

——………

"Ohhh, Goood, ohhhhh, Goooood!"

Meanwhile, Steph, walking through the corridors of the castle with rigid shoulders. Furious at having been called a mere jack-off toy—no. *At herself for being hurt by that*—she screamed indiscriminately.

"Ohhh, God, I knew it, this feeling is an illusion brought on by the covenant—it's a manner of curse!"

But Steph didn't notice…

"That beast! That pedophile! There's no way I should love him. It must be the covenant."

…That Sora had suggested releasing her from the covenant. That is to say, the solution of playing another game and saying, "Don't love me." And she'd ignored it completely, and even forgotten about it.

And what that meant—

⏻ EPILOGUE

—Reception Chamber, Elkia Royal Castle. On the single throne sat two, playing a DSP game. A black-haired young man in jeans and an "I ♥ PPL" T-shirt, with the queen's tiara wrapped around his arm. A white-skinned, long-haired girl with red eyes in a black sailor suit, with the king's crown tying up her hair. In fact—they were this country's king—Sora—and queen—Shiro—the siblings.

"I'm *telling* you, we're going naked and you're setting off traps? That's ridiculous."

"…For efficiency."

"If you want efficiency, then why are we playing naked? Let's play for real, d00d!"

"…That would just…waste time; it wouldn't be…fun."

They'd brought a large volume of games to this world. But they were all games they'd literally *maxed out*. Which meant it was questionable whether they were even good for killing time. But there was a reason they were killing time. It was—

"I'm—done changing…"

Hearing her voice, the two immediately sleeved their game and took out their phones. The one who had appeared was a beautiful girl with auburn hair and features suggesting refinement—but.

Wearing a maid outfit that was just revealing enough—not excessively tacky. Stephanie Dola...the blood kin of the previous king, former royalty—and now...

To Steph, appearing with her face bright red, Sora nevertheless asked:

"Mm? Is it revealing enough to blush over?"

"...I didn't let her wear underwear..."

"C-could you not spell that out?!"

The cry of Steph.

—Indeed. These two leaders were exploring the boundaries of R-18. Seeing herself a slave of love—no, probably by now *no more than the plaything of the two*—Steph looked up at the ceiling in self-hatred.

"Ahh, the *obviously not wearing any* effect so prevalent in two-dimensional imagery."

"...Mm...but it doesn't quite do it."

"You're right, Director. We can't move frame by frame like in 2-D; it's most inconvenient."

"...Should we strip her?"

"Hmm, Steph. Can you show some more skin without revealing your nipples or other juicy bits?"

"Don't call them *juicy bits*!"

"...And then, pop."

"No. That's not okay when she's *not wearing any*, Director."

"...Don't worry...I anticipated this—and used bandages."

"Umn......mng? Uh, well...hng? I don't think that's okay."

"...Then what about a very small swimsuit...not okay?"

"—Hm, now that you mention it. But, Director, by that logic, it would be okay for her to be totally naked if she was wearing bandages."

"...Mmg...All Ages is hard."

Reclining his back on the throne, Sora said in a small voice:

"But then, no matter how close to the edge we record her, I'm never actually gonna get off, am I; instead, I'm just gonna get more and more frustrated..."

But Shiro, her ears sharp enough to pick it up, said.

"...I...don't mind; go ahead."

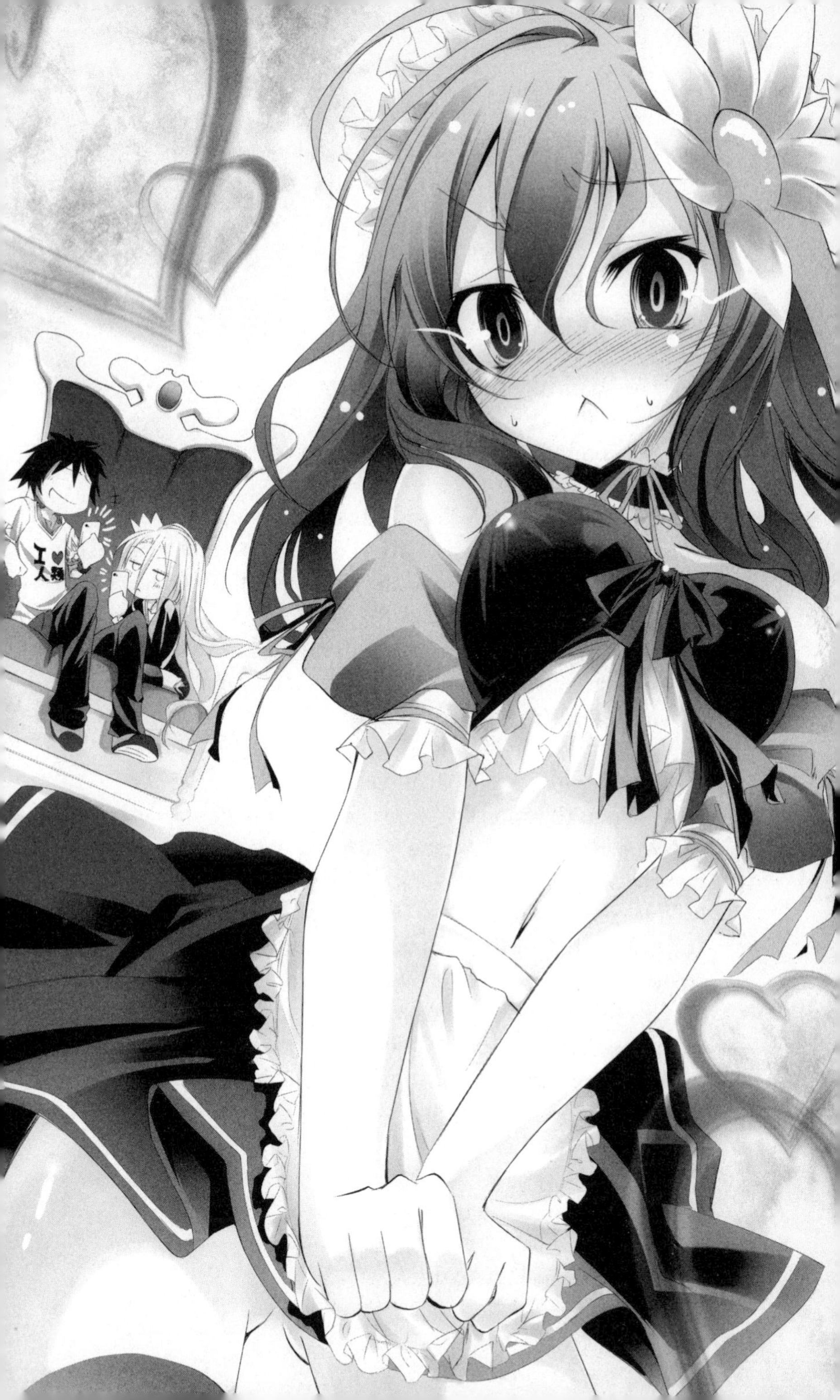

"Hey, actually? Your brother isn't an exhibitionist."

"…Don't worry… I won't look…just like at home."

"Hng? Wait, hold on there, I always waited until I saw you were asleep first!"

"…Your rustling around…wakes me up."

"I can't—were you always awake?!"

Sora, holding his face, beet-red.

"Omigawd! I'm, like, totally ruined now!"

"…It's okay. I'll take damaged goods."

The sister comforted him, patting him on the shoulder.

"And—then—"

"If *you're* totally ruined, what does that make *me* after you've made me go around like this!" Steph, who'd been meanwhile shaking her shoulders, shouted out, and then continued as if having reached her limit.

"And anyway, you make me handle the procedures for the coronation and the succession, you make me stay up through three nights, and then you call me out and it's this! God, you think you're so great!"

"…We are the monarch… That makes us great.…"

On Shiro's quite reasonable words, Sora continued casually.

"We've been up three days, too, you know. We can do two more or so, no problem."

"Playing games, right?!"

"Yes, games. The job of the monarch, in this world."

"Hngk…"

Indeed—in this world, where everything was decided by games—*even national borders*—being good at games was a condition for being a monarch, and it was justifiable to call this training.

"Man… Here we can just play games all day and people call it a real job; this place is heaven."

At Sora's burbling as if he had found Shangri-La, Steph shouted:

"No, we don't! You've got domestic affairs you should be taking care of!"

"Mm? You finished the succession?"

"Yes, I just did, before you called me!"

"That's what I was waiting for. I'm the type who likes to get the *domestic affairs* done all at once in *Civ*."

With that, he shifted Shiro aside and stood from the throne.

"So—will you call the ministers?"

■■■

Before the ministers who gathered in the Great Assembly Hall. Sora and Shiro, rising to the podium—. But they interrupted all kinds of reports to lay out:

"I have something to tell you first."

Looking around at the faces of everyone, Sora—*the king of the human race*—spoke again, carefully.

"As you all know, Immanity currently finds itself in a tight spot. Given that we mean to take the offensive, *we have no room to look behind us*. As such, to eliminate concerns for the future—we shall play rock-paper-scissors."

Swinging his open hand above his head, he announced in a ringing voice to the attentive ministers:

"The wager is the state of being prohibited hereafter from making any false reports, including selective or manipulative communication of information... We shall play a game by the Covenants, and you shall *intentionally lose* to form a contract."

Taking advantage of the "absolutely binding" rule written in the Covenants by *throwing a match*.

With his face asking why no one had thought of something so simple, Sora continued:

"And, so, my good subjects, let us remember that the fate of the human race rests on our shoulders as we play this game—I shall throw scissors, and all of you shall throw paper; lose purposefully and prove your loyalty. Incidentally, if there be any among you who, *slighting the powers of observation and memory of the siblings before you, has a mind to reject the setup and the contract*, I suggest you leave now."

—Thus having warned them from trying to resist the covenant by pretending to lose, Sora sang out—

"*Aschente.*"

"*—Aschente!*"

As the swearing of the contract echoed, they began their rock-paper-scissors. And, thus—the contract was concluded.

"...So, then, let's start with the Minister of Agriculture—your report."

"Your Majesty—our country is currently facing a dire situation in regard to food."

Listening to the explanation of the system of farming, its management, and allocation of taxes, etc. After it was all finished, Sora nodded once.

"I have understood... Then implement the measures I shall henceforth state."

"...Yes, Sir."

"Regarding production—you shall introduce *crop rotation*."

"—Can you explain, Sir?"

"On a single field, rotate in order between cultivating winter cereals such as wheat, root vegetables such as turnips and beets, summer cereals such as rye, and forage crops such as clover, which serve to restore the fertility of the soil. This will lead to decreased cropping of cereals, but increased cropping of root vegetables and legumes. In particular, introducing the cultivation of turnips and the like will resolve fodder shortages and enable livestock to be raised through the winter. Further, the soil-regenerative properties of the manure and the forage crops will eliminate the need to leave fields fallow."

Sora spouted it off as if it were obvious. All in presence could only stand speechless at the revolutionary proposals of their king. Moreover—.

"Keys to success in this plan shall be a concentrated labor force and gathering of scattered croplands into specific areas. These policies may put some small- and midscale farmers out of work, but production of food will improve by a factor of four or more. Implement these instructions with the highest priority."

He'd even pointed out the potential issues.

"Wh-what about the budget?"

"We shall issue *bonds* for purchase by banks—but please entrust this matter to the Minister of Economy."

"—A-as you wish, Sir."

"Next, we must address the unemployment resulting from this plan. Minister of Economy, Minister of Industry, your reports—"

————……

In this manner. Regarding the king who proposed groundbreaking reforms to solve all kinds of problems one after the other. In a meeting lasting only four hours. Among the ministers, it came to be whispered that he was *the wisest king in human history.*

…Playing with the tablet he held, Sora said:

"Man, I sure was right to download all those reference books for quiz game study gramming."

On his tablet were over *forty thousand* books of an academic nature. From math, science, astronomy, physics, and engineering to medicine, history, and military tactics. Even data extracted and saved from that good old wiki professor—in other words, he had *most of the knowledge of the human race as of the early twenty-first century.*

"…Brother, you're always so shady… That's cheating."

Though Shiro pointed this out, with her usual half-closed eyes, Sora knitted his brow.

"Considering we're in a world with an official cheat like magic, would you not call me a cheater just for introducing a little technology from another world? And, come on, these domestic affairs are kind of urgent, aren't they?"

…That said, introducing too much future technology at once could cause unexpected strains. To be honest, he did want to introduce "electrical engineering" sooner than later, but…

"If we could just make cameras and mics, it would probably help some in fighting magic."

Their current situation, with only two phones with useless antennas, could hardly be seen as comfortable. Perhaps they should, after all, start looking for a way to contact the Flügel and—

—Steph appeared softly in the Assembly Hall, still wearing her skimpy maid outfit. That is—just as Shiro and Sora had made her dress and then left her.

"……Sora—no. Y-Your Majesty…you have a visitor."

"——Damn, you greeted a visitor in that getup? You've got guts."

"…Steph, you're amazing."

"If it's okay for me to change, why didn't you say so! *Wwaaaugh!*"

Covering his ears from the weeping scream of Steph, Sora waved his hand.

"Ohh, yeah, sorry, sorry; so, go hurry up and fix yourself. Jeez, people are going to wonder about the quality of our country."

"People are going to wonder about the quality of your head!"

However, without waiting for Steph's guidance, a voice rang through the Assembly Hall.

"Aha-ha-ha-ha, it seems like you're having a lot of fun here!"

Into the Great Assembly Hall, where Sora and Shiro, Steph, and the ministers were assembled. *Tk, tk*—walked a boy. Sora and Shiro recognized his face. It was unmistakable. He was the one—stretching his hands out of the computer—who had brought them into this world—

"…Well, if it isn't the *so-called God*. How's it hanging?"

"Oh, you. I'm not 'so-called'; I *am* God."

Scratching his head, *aha-ha*, the boy spoke.

"Come to think of it, I think I forgot to tell you my name—

"**—Tet…that's my name. It's a pleasure, Blank.**"

Wham———*!* As soon as the boy said, "Tet," the atmosphere in the room changed. The impact of the holy name? Everyone except two (Shiro and Sora) found their pores opening and sweat blasting out. The ministers shook with faces drained of blood, Steph with a body on the verge of collapsing. Yet without his seeming to take a whit of notice of them.

"What you think of *my world*? Does it tickle your fancy?"

"Yeah, you've got a great aesthetic. Our God ought to take some lessons from you."

"…*Nod, nod.*"

Watching Sora and Shiro sassing God, everyone around felt their hearts squeezed almost hard enough to rupture.

—The one standing before them was the One True God—Tet. He who had *the authority to erase the world and make a new one on a whim*. But Tet himself just smiled back with no sign of concern.

"I'm glad to hear it. So…it looks like the crisis to the survival of Immanity has been averted for now."

"Yep, just as you wanted."

Everyone made faces that said, *Huh?*

"As if it *just so happened* that the nearest city *just so happened* to be the last human country, and it *just so happened* to be competing to decide the monarch…right. Come on, you're not gonna try to tell me all that was a coincidence, are you?"

To Sora's brazen speech, the God replied with a joyful smile.

"Aha-ha… But don't get the wrong idea. My philosophy is basically to be an *observer*; I don't support any particular race—but, yeah, I guess I'll admit in this case I had some personal feelings involved."

The boy—Tet—kicked the ground and pouted as if bored. He said:

"I wonder if you remember what I said…you know—that everything is decided by games in this world."

—*Yeah*. Sora grasped the intent behind his words and said it preemptively.

"…I see. So *even the throne of the One True God is decided by games.*"

"—Wha—"

—Everyone around could only gasp this, except Shiro, who seemed impressed. And Tet alone smiled mirthfully and spoke.

"That's right! That's why I made it so there are 'sixteen seeds.'"

With a click——everything came together in Sora's head. "Ixseeds"— the chessboard beyond the horizon—*the God who said he lived over there*. The number of pieces on one side of a chessboard—sixteen. Meaning.

"…You *rule over all the races as a champion*—so there's a *challenge against the God* on the table."

Tet smiled pleasantly and replied:

"What a nimble mind you have. You're so adaptable, it's hard to believe you just came from another world."

"Well, thank you!"

"I mean it. But even though I was looking forward to playing a game with my title as God at stake, I got stuck for thousands of years with nothing to do. So, when I was *wandering around* another world, I happened to hear the rumors about you guys—Blank."

With a sense of excitement and deep interest, the God looked at Sora and Shiro and said:

"You know, the rumors about the gamer always at the top of all kinds of games, which they were even starting to call an urban legend."

To God's smile, Sora grinned back.

"Hey, God, should you be smiling?"

"Huh?"

"You knew about us when you summoned us to this world. You knew our—Blank's—policy: *We always stand at the top of any game.* Right?"

"Yeah, of course."

And then the God grinned back.

"That's why I figured that you guys would definitely—*come to win the right to challenge me.*"

Everyone around froze. It meant—to say nothing of the greatest country in the world—Elf, Rank Seven. They aimed even for Old Deus and Phantasma: for Rank One. Which meant—to conquer and control all the Ixseeds. It was no longer a question on the level of world conquest—

"...So, God, let me ask you one more time. Should you be smiling?

"Don't you remember that you've *lost to us once already*?"

—And, this time, truly, none could believe their ears.

——The God lost?

———To the mere humans here?

But Tet laughed it off.

"Heh-heh, I'm sure you've grasped this well already, but the games in this world are a whole different story from some online chess game in your world. It's true that I lost to you siblings at *'normal chess'*—that's why I summoned you here. But...next time, I'm not gonna lose!"

With that, Sora and Shiro. Both siblings seeming to grasp something together. Looked at each other and smiled.

"—Hey, God."

But God—answered genially:

"Just call me Tet. What is it?"

"Okay, Tet—you'd never lost before, had you?"

At that simple question. Tet's smile thinned into an impudent grin.

"*The God of Play—lost for the first time.* And he was so mad, so mad he couldn't stand it. And so he summoned us to this world—— to beat us 'playing by this world's rules this time.' Am I right?"

"Heh-heh... How interesting. What makes you think that?"

Tet put the question to them, keeping his smile up on the surface.

"Because we know *just* how you feel. Blank has not a single loss— but we've lost to each other over and over."

"...But we don't let each other quit while they're ahead."

"As a result, my pure-genius sister is specialized in games themselves."

"...Brother's gotten better...but only at dirty tricks."

"Hey, what do you mean, 'dirty'? Diplomacy is part of the game."

"...Cheating is cowardly."

"It's fine as long as no one catches you! That's how it works in this world, too, right?!"

At this sibling banter, Tet laughed heartily, while everyone but the siblings cowered before him.

"Ah-ha-ha-ha-ha-ha. Yeah, I was right to summon you two. You're right; *I'm not gonna let you quit while you're ahead.* Next time, I'm gonna win—basically, that's why I summoned you. Are you disappointed in me?"

"Nah? I'm more relieved that it wasn't some lofty reason like *save the human race.* So, have you descended from the heavens today just to tell us that? You really *are* bored."

"Nah, I came to thank you.

"After you guys—Immanity—took down Elven Gard, albeit indirectly, the whole world's gotten anxious, just as you planned.— It seems the Eastern Union takes an interest in that 'phone' you showed them, and they can't sleep at night thinking about what country might be behind it. I wonder why? There's also another ball of curiosity, Avant Heim, that is fascinated with the technology you used to defeat Elven Gard. Meanwhile, Elven Gard themselves are rushing to identify what country has this technology that beat them. If they knew you actually smashed them head-on, without cheating—ha-ha, with those guys, you might get *dissected*."

Thus—having been generously provided information by Tet, Sora, suspiciously:

"Didn't you say you *don't support any particular race*?"

"Sure, so, this is just by way of thanks. This world was getting boring, so I'm giving you information as thanks for heating it up again. This is the first and last time, so use it well."

Smiling, taking a step back without turning, Tet continued.

"All right, it seems like if I stick around, you guys are never gonna be able to relax, so I'll take my leave. See ya!"

As this *God* made to leave, Sora and Shiro spoke up:

"Hey, Tet."

"Yeah?"

"Thanks for giving us a new life. You were right—this world is where we belong."

"…Thank you, God."

And, this time, all three spoke together.

"""…See you soon.—Next time, on the chessboard.""""

—And then, Tet disappeared, as if melting into the air. Everyone let out all their breath, as if they were finally permitted to breathe.

—Have you heard a rumor that goes like this?

"*Hh…* That's one amusing God we've got here."

"…I want to play…him again."

—A gamer set unbeatable records in the online rankings for all kinds of games and swept up all the top ranks.

—But one day the gamer suddenly disappeared.

—The accelerating *urban legend* ultimately rose to the status of a *myth*.

"Th-th-that—w-w-was the One True God?!"

"Y-Your Majesty! I-is it true that you vanquished the God?"

"Wait, we should really be worried about the Eastern Union; they're—"

"You mean Elven Gard! If our king and queen were to be targeted personally—"

—And now, the story that had stopped and become myth in *that world*…

—saw its continuation, in a new setting, a world called *Disboard*.

"Ahhh, shut uuup! Don't all talk at once!"

"…Brother."

"Yeah, I know—"

Sora rose to the podium, then leapt upon the table in the center, spreading his arms, and spoke to all assembled.

—Now, as a convention.

—And as a grace, I'd like to open as follows:

—Once upon a time—.

"Come—let the games begin. Let us make the objective: Overthrow the God!"

—Now then, let me tell you *the newest myth*.

⏻ AFTERWORD

Ohhhh, yeah—this is it! I've always wanted to write one of these—an "Afterword"! Nice to meet you. I've always been the guy doing the illustrations, and I've always wanted to try sitting in the author's seat and writing the afterword, and, today, my dream has finally come true—I'm the author *and* illustrator, Yuu Kamiya. Umm, so, originally, I'm a *manga-ka*. Uh, yeah, I'm...on leave, as they say... I've come down with a bit of a nasty illness, so I have to take a break from drawing manga, which is very demanding. Plus, now, thanks to *Itsuka Tenma no Kuro-usagi* (*A Dark Rabbit Has Seven Lives*; published under the Fantasia Bunko imprint), I might even be better known as an illustrator than as a *manga-ka* now...and now that I've started writing novels, too, what am I "originally," anyway... A-anyway, I'm *also* a *manga-ka*! And *No Game No Life* is my novel debut. Actually, I originally conceived of it as a manga. I wasn't going to be the one drawing it; it was *for* someone—I just meant to be the "Story by" guy. The person who was supposed to draw it told me:

"I love fantasy, but I can't stand battles!"

—and, knowing how ~~tediou~~ hard it is to draw battle manga, I wanted to grant that wish! "So, what about a fantasy world where you *can't* battle!" I thought. And combined with games, that to which I devoted all my waking, nonworking hours!

"A world where even national borders are decided by games—by *play for dominion!*"

So, with this upside-down idea, I took my personal interests full throttle to make this. But unfortunately, the project never reached fruition. Thinking, I sure would like to realize this one day, I was left with a plot and a bunch of notes. Then, after that, I was forced to take a break from manga due to a troublesome physical condition. I was super-vegetating in the hospital ~~and they didn't even let me bring in my games~~, and, man—

—**This is not your appointed time to die as a creator.**

…What? It's not that old. It still works; don't give up on it. S-so, anyway, while I was lying there in the hospital, I made a lot of changes to the plot to make it convenient as a novel series, I mean, perfect. And, now, here it—hey, come to think of it, my editor was saying—"There are people who decide whether to buy based on the afterword, so sell," or something like that. Okay—how's this look?

No Game No Life

Two siblings. Gaming was their only skill.
And then the two failures at life found themselves—

—in a world without war, where games decide everything.

—COME ON...

...STAKE IT ALL, EVERY-THING YOU HAVE.

Sister—Shiro
11/Awkward/Shut-in

A world where gambling decides lives—even borders.

NOOO! THERE'S NO CHANCE FOR IMMANITY TO WIN AGAINST..

...ELVEN MAGIC!

Stephanie Dola
18/Victim/Royalty (?)

The enemy—*Ixseeds*—use magic and powers—

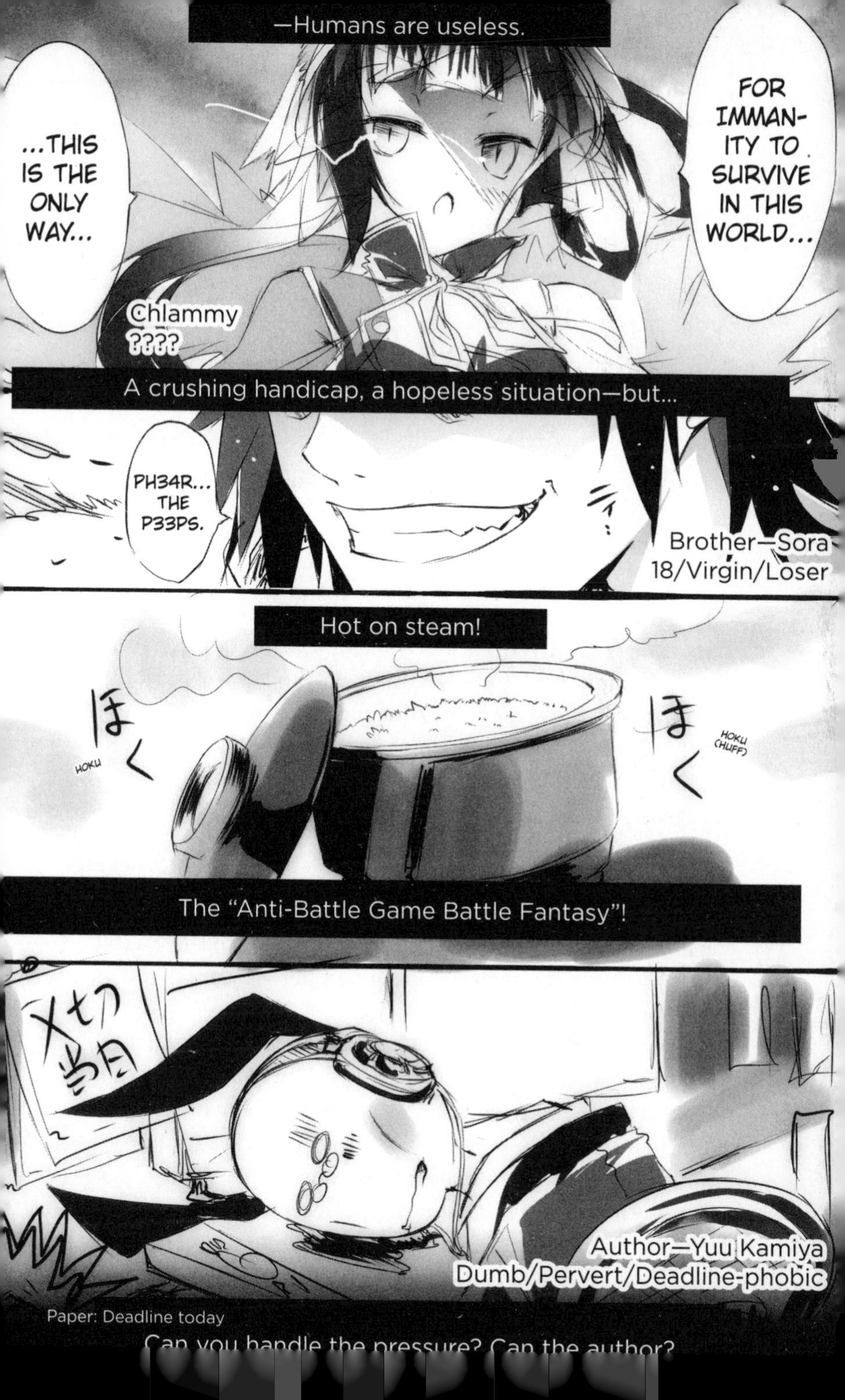
—Humans are useless.
FOR IMMAN-ITY TO SURVIVE IN THIS WORLD...
...THIS IS THE ONLY WAY...
Chlammy
????
A crushing handicap, a hopeless situation—but...
PH34R... THE P33PS.
Brother—Sora
18/Virgin/Loser
Hot on steam!
ほく
HOKU (HUFF)
ほく
HOKU
The "Anti-Battle Game Battle Fantasy"!
Author—Yuu Kamiya
Dumb/Pervert/Deadline-phobic
Paper: Deadline today
Can you handle the pressure? Can the author?

(*convincingly*) Yeah—that's pretty much what the book is like.

—Or it could be false advertising on the level of a Hollywood movie trailer? Those of you reading the afterword first will just have to read the book to find out. For those of you who are reading it last—umm. Yeah, well. If it sells well enough to make into a comic, let's just consider that the flag for me to draw it and laugh and—

"Mr. Kamiya, Mr. Kamiya."

—Huh? Oh, what is it, Editor S?

"Shall we start looking for someone to draw the comic? After all, you have a track record when it comes to *manga*, and—"

Aha-ha, sorry about that, my signal's not very good and I can't hear you.

"Actually, in the first place, what are you trying to do, saying, 'I can't draw manga due to my health, so I want to try writing a novel, since that's less demanding,' and then drawing a manga in the back of the book?"

You're the one who told me to draw one!

"Huh? All I said was, 'It's almost unprecedented for the author and illustrator to be the same person who's also a *manga-ka*, so please take advantage of that to sell the book'?"

—Are you telling me I should interpret that otherwise than "Draw a manga"?

"I didn't say so *explicitly*!"

Hmm. For a moment there, my editor's character reminded me of our protagonists. Maybe I should have emphasized Stephanie's hatred more!

Oh, come to think of it. This is coming out the **same month** as Takaya Kagami's ***Itsuka Tenma no Kuro-usagi*, Volume 10: *Koutei de Warau Majo* (A Witch Smiles in the Schoolyard)**, for which I also did the illustrations! I put supereffort into that as well, so *please* buy it; you *must*!

…*Hff*, so, as I write this. I'm still not totally done yet. And, actually, right now—*I'm in Brazil.* For the health reasons alluded to above, I'm back in my home country for a time. Actually, the text and illustrations of this *No Game No Life* volume. And the illustrations for the new volume of *ItsuTen*, mentioned above, were almost all composed in Brazil.

—A big trunk filled with my LCD tablet and PC and a huge load of packing materials.

"The purpose of your trip?"

Medical reasons.

"What's all this equipment for?"

Work.

…Well, it shouldn't be too hard to imagine the trouble I went through at customs.

—Yeah, it's crazy, right? I'm a sick goddamn guy. What am I doing getting cared for on the other side of the world while answering two companies as they badger me for delivery?

"Excuse me, Mr. Kamiya."

Yes? What is it, Editor S for "*sadist*"?

"Um, I'm more of a masochist, really—Mr. Fujimi and I explained the schedule to you in advance, didn't we?"

I don't remember *agreeing*!

"Well, I don't know what to tell you…"

Anyway, when you call me *the day before the New Year's Eve*

Comiket, when I'm making the final sprint in the middle of all that end-of-year insanity, of course I would feel like sending you off with what you want to hear!

"Um, well, frankly, that's entirely your—"

Editor S's epic sadism aside. Heh, that's the successor to Takaya Kagami's previous editor, Catherine, all right… That was an ambush no matter how you look at it. Pouncing on me when I'm mentally unsound—……

So…is this a good time?

"——Uh, for what?"

An *extension*. ♥

"Uhhh… I didn't quite get that; must be the sig—"

Hmm, come to think of it, who was it who let me put the text on a diet by eight pages to achieve the desired page count and then announced *the same day* I got back to Japan, **"I forgot to account for the ten black-and-white illustrations"**?

"…Can't you *pretend that never happened*?"

If you cut this out in editing, I'll *tweet on you!* ♥

"I, Editor S, most humbly and sincerely apologize and ask forgiveness for my failure and indiscretion in not only greatly inconveniencing you by my own grave error, but furthermore expecting you, the author, the great Yuu Kamiya, to clean up the mess I made."

—Yes, now that I've succeeded in paying back a *grown-up*, I hope to meet you again in the next volume; farewell!

"Oh, by the way. Mr. Kamiya, when will you have the manuscript for the second volume ready? Mr. Kamiya? Are you there? Hello?"

IXSEED RANK 14:
WEREBEAST

IN NO GAME NO LIFE, VOL. 7— FACING THE GREAT COUNTRIES OF AVANT HEIM AND THE EASTERN UNION, CAN MERE HUMANS LIKE " " CONTINUE THEIR NO-LOSS RECORD—?

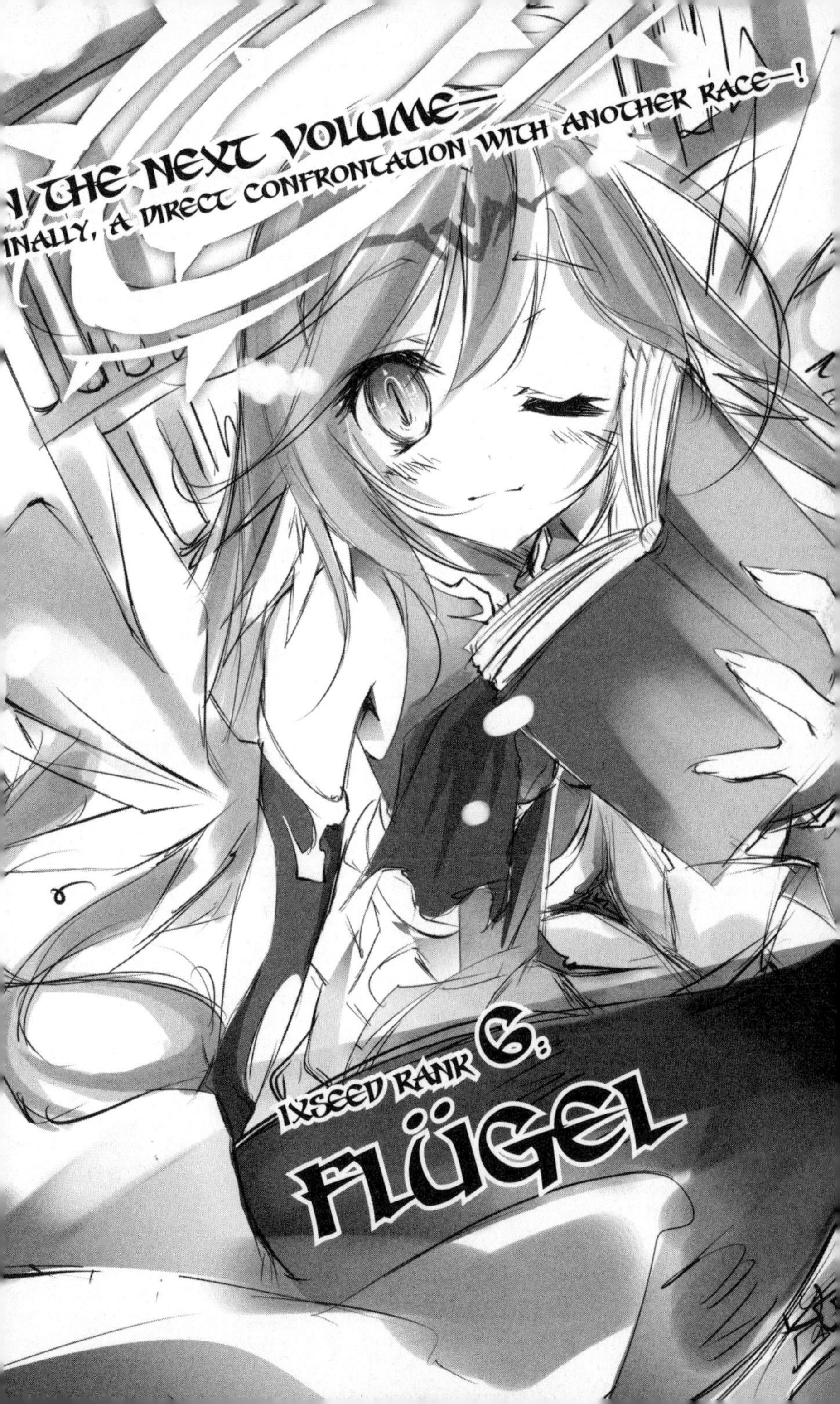

N THE NEXT VOLUME—
INALLY, A DIRECT CONFRONTATION WITH ANOTHER RACE—!
IXSEED RANK 6.
FLÜGEL

No Game No Life

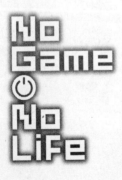

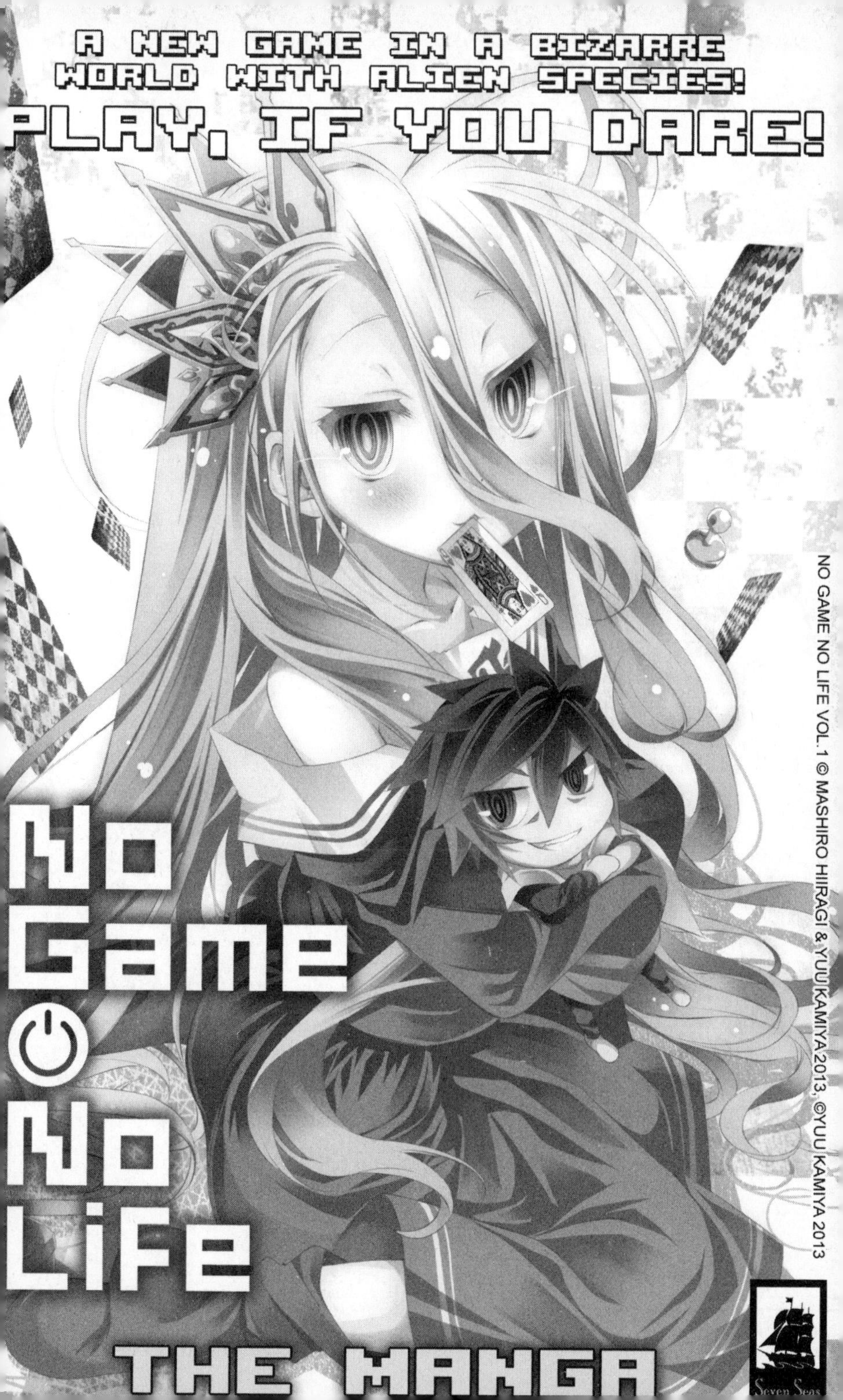
A NEW GAME IN A BIZARRE WORLD WITH ALIEN SPECIES!
PLAY, IF YOU DARE!
No Game No Life
THE MANGA
NO GAME NO LIFE VOL. 1 © MASHIRO HIIRAGI & YUU KAMIYA 2013, ©YUU KAMIYA 2013
Seven Seas